A Dangerous Game . . .

"That reminds me," said Gabe. "You haven't set a fire yet, Nick."

"What?" Nick gaped at him. "What are you talking about?"

"Max set a fire," Gabe went on. "He proved he's got guts."

"Good for him," said Nick. "I don't have to prove anything."

"Or maybe you're afraid," said Gabe deliberately.

For a moment no one said anything. Gabe's gone too far, Jill thought. But Nick just took a deep breath and held it, then turned. "Come on," he said. "Let's go."

"Maybe you're right, Nick," Gabe said with exaggerated kindness. "Maybe it's not your turn yet. It's my turn. . . ."

"What about that shack over there?" said Max, pointing to a rundown wooden shack.

"Hey, man," said Nick nervously. "You're not really going to do it, are you?"

"You don't think so?" said Gabe. He clicked on the lighter. "Just watch me."

Books by R. L. Stine

Fear Street: THE NEW GIRL
Fear Street: THE SURPRISE PARTY
Fear Street: THE OVERNIGHT
Fear Street: MISSING
Fear Street: THE WRONG NUMBER
Fear Street: THE SLEEPWALKER
Fear Street: HAUNTED
Fear Street: HALLOWEEN PARTY
Fear Street: THE STEPSISTER
Fear Street: SKI WEEKEND
Fear Street: THE FIRE GAME
Fear Street: LIGHTS OUT
Fear Street: THE SECRET BEDROOM
Fear Street: THE KNIFE
Fear Street: PROM QUEEN
Fear Street: FIRST DATE
Fear Street: THE BEST FRIEND

Fear Street Super Chiller: PARTY SUMMER
Fear Street Super Chiller: SILENT NIGHT
Fear Street Super Chiller: GOODNIGHT KISS
Fear Street Super Chiller: BROKEN HEARTS

Fear Street CHEERLEADERS: THE FIRST EVIL
Fear Street CHEERLEADERS: THE SECOND EVIL
Fear Street CHEERLEADERS: THE THIRD EVIL

HOW I BROKE UP WITH ERNIE
PHONE CALLS
CURTAINS
BROKEN DATE

Available from ARCHWAY Paperbacks

FEAR STREET
R·L·STINE

The Fire Game

AN ARCHWAY PAPERBACK
Published by POCKET BOOKS
New York   London   Toronto   Sydney   Tokyo   Singapore

AN ARCHWAY PAPERBACK *Original*

An Archway Paperback published by
POCKET BOOKS, a division of Simon & Schuster Inc.
1230 Avenue of the Americas, New York, NY 10020

ISBN: 0-671-72481-9

First Archway Paperback printing March 1991

15 14 13 12 11 10 9 8 7 6

FEAR STREET is a registered trademark of Parachute Press, Inc.

AN ARCHWAY PAPERBACK and colophon are registered trademarks of Simon & Schuster Inc.

Cover art by Bill Schmidt

Printed in the U.S.A.

IL 6+

The Fire Game

chapter

1

*F*leecy clouds moved across the sun, then suddenly broke up, sending glittering sunlight through the dusty library window. Jill Franks squinted against the sudden brightness, then laughed as her friend Andrea Hubbard quickly put on oversize purple sunglasses with heart-shaped frames.

"Where'd you get those?" Jill whispered.

"Aren't they great?" exclaimed Andrea. "Don't you think they make me look sexy and mysterious?"

"Will you guys keep it down?" Both Jill and Andrea turned back in surprise to Diane Hamilton, the only one of the three who actually had a book open. The girls were at their favorite study table behind the stacks in the school library.

"What did you say?" shouted Andrea, and she and Jill cracked up again.

"The glasses look great," said Diane, trying not to laugh. "But, Andrea, this *is* a library. And we're supposed to be studying for the geography quiz."

"Relax," said Jill. "We're the only people in here. Miss Dotson went to lunch fifteen minutes ago."

"Besides," said Andrea, stretching like a cat, "the quiz is two hours away. Maybe we'll be captured by aliens before sixth period."

Jill laughed again. Andrea never took anything seriously. Jill sometimes wondered if it was just a pose, or if Andrea really did see everything as a joke.

"It's easy for you to say," said Diane. "Both of you have been in this school system your whole lives. But at my old school we never studied geography."

"Ooh, poor baby," said Andrea sarcastically. "And I bet you still think the world's flat."

"Who says it isn't?" said Jill.

"Come on, you two," urged Diane. "I really have to do well this semester." A serious look clouded her small, heart-shaped face, as if the geography quiz were the most important thing in her life.

Jill studied Diane with a mixture of exasperation and affection. The shy, petite brown-haired girl contrasted oddly with Jill and Andrea. Tall, slim Jill, with her long, thick black hair, and bouncy, muscular Andrea, with her boy-short red hair, were both outgoing and ready to laugh at anything. But when Diane had joined the gymnastics team at the beginning of the semester, the three had hit it off right away, anyway.

Maybe, Jill thought, it was because Diane was so different. She was as calm as Andrea was volatile, and as serious as Jill was bubbly, and she was the sweetest person Jill had ever known, always ready with a compliment or a word of encouragement.

"Hey, don't worry about the quiz," said Andrea.

"Mrs. Markham never counts quizzes for the final grade."

"That's not what *she* said," Diane protested.

"Who cares?" asked Andrea. "I only care about getting good enough grades to keep my sports eligibility."

"After you win the state gymnastics championship, nobody will care what your grades are," said Jill.

"Do you really think I have a chance to win?" asked Andrea.

"Who else?" said Jill.

"Well, how about the twelve other finalists?" Andrea said.

"I'll bet none of them is as good as you," said Diane. "In fact, you're the best I've ever seen on the floor routine."

"Thanks for saying so," said Andrea. "I shouldn't admit it, but I think I do have a chance for a medal. I just wish I were a little stronger on the balance beam."

"We'll help you practice this weekend," said Jill. "Won't we, Diane?"

"Sure," said Diane, her serious face transformed by a smile.

"What I really need help with is picking the music for my floor routine," Andrea said. "Any ideas?"

"How about *Bolero?*" said Jill. *Bolero* was one of her favorite pieces.

"No way. Too many other girls use it," said Andrea. "I'd like to have something really different, something no one else would think of using."

"How about some original music?" said Diane suddenly.

"Oh, sure," said Andrea. "What do you have in

mind—the two of you humming on combs while I do my flips?"

"I was just thinking," Diane said, sounding excited. "I have this friend—he's kind of a songwriter. I mean, he writes his own songs and plays them on the guitar. He's really good."

"Great, maybe he'd like to sit on the uneven parallel bars and strum away." Andrea sighed. "I'm serious about this. I need something really special."

"I'm serious too," said Diane, sounding hurt.

"I think Diane's idea is great," said Jill. "If her friend came up with something neat, we could tape it for the competition. For sure no one else will be using original music."

"You really think he'd do it?" said Andrea.

"You can ask him yourself, next week," said Diane. "His father just got transferred to Shadyside, and Gabe and his mother will be here in a few days."

"Gabe?" said Andrea.

"Yeah. It's short for Gabriel," said Diane. "Like the angel. Only Gabe's more of a devil."

Jill and Andrea both stared at Diane for a moment, because that didn't sound like her type of friend at all.

"What do you mean?" said Jill.

"He's not like other boys," said Diane. "He's—well, a little wild and kind of funny and sweet all at once. I've known him practically my whole life, and I never have any idea what he's going to do."

"Sounds interesting," said Andrea, arching one thin, dark eyebrow.

"He's also good-looking," Diane added as an afterthought. "He's got the greenest eyes you ever saw. I mean really green green, not brownish."

"So when do we meet Mr. Perfect?" asked Andrea.

"As I said, he and his mom should be here any day now. I'm really excited they're coming, but . . ." Diane let her thought trail off.

"But?" said Jill. "What's the but?"

"Well, Gabe's a little worried about moving to a small town," Diane said. "He's lived in the city his whole life."

"We'll just have to make it interesting for him," said Andrea. "First of all, we'll keep him away from Nick and Max."

"Come on, Andrea," said Jill. "They're not so bad."

"Then why won't you go out with them?" countered Andrea. "Everyone knows they're both crazy about you."

"Get real," Jill said, but she knew what Andrea meant. Nick Malone and Max Bogner had been hanging out with the girls ever since the past summer. Both boys were nice, but *exciting* would be the last word anyone would use to describe either of them.

Officially they were all just friends, but Jill knew Andrea was right, both Nick and Max were interested in her. Too bad she wasn't interested in either of them. Maybe this new boy—Gabe—would be someone she could care about.

She was jolted from her thoughts by a diabolical cackle, and a moment later Nick, his long, skinny fingers twisted into claws, emerged from behind a tall bookshelf.

"Ah, zere zey are," he said in a terrible Dracula accent. "My favorite leetle morsels."

"Maybe we can wrap zem up here and ship zem back to ze castle," said Max in the same accent. He was as stocky and round as Nick was long and skinny, and his plump, reddish face was screwed up into such a ridiculous horror-movie expression that all three girls laughed out loud.

"Don't tell me—you guys have been renting ancient horror movies again," said Jill.

"How did you guess?" said Max, making the face again.

"We saw three last night," said Nick, sitting on the windowsill by the table. "They were all cool, but the best one was called *The Torch*. You ever see it?"

"We have better things to do with our IQs," said Andrea in a bored voice. "For you two, it may be too late."

Nick ignored the insult and went on. "It's about this guy who can make fire come out of the tips of his fingers. Like a human flame thrower."

"Sounds like a handy guy to take on a barbecue," said Andrea.

"Yeah," said Nick. "Anyway, he's a good guy, but then he runs across a bad guy who can do the same thing, and pretty soon they're having these big fire duels."

"Like this!" said Max, suddenly flicking on a disposable butane lighter. He turned it on high so that the flame shot up, then aimed it in Nick's direction.

"Hey!" said Nick, still laughing. He reached into his pocket and pulled out a lighter of his own. "Take that, Torch Scum!" he said and swiped his lighter at Max. In the next instant the two boys were faking a duel with the lighters.

Jill and Andrea both started laughing, because the boys were so ridiculous. But then Jill became aware of Diane's chair suddenly scraping away from them.

"Don't," Diane whispered fiercely. "Don't," she repeated more loudly. *"Don't!"*

Jill turned to her friend and saw that Diane's pretty face was twisted in fear.

"Stop them, Jill. Make them stop!" Diane gripped Jill's arm.

"They're only fooling around," Jill said. She did talk to the guys, though. "Hey, chill out, will you?"

"No. Keep it up," said Andrea. "Maybe you can start a fire and get the geography quiz canceled."

"I only use my powers in the service of good," said Max. "And geography is— Hey, watch out!"

Max stepped aside as Nick lunged at him. Nick's gawky body fell against the side of the stacks, knocking several books to the floor. Before he regained his balance, he had landed in Andrea's lap.

"Get off me!" grunted Andrea.

"May I have this dance?" Nick asked. He straightened up and leaned against the wall, still flicking his lighter.

"Cut it out, you dweeb," said Jill. She knew the boys were only fooling around, but she suddenly realized how many flammable things the library contained.

Nick picked up an empty folder and repeatedly brought the flame close to it, then pulled it away.

"No!" shrieked Diane in a panic. Everyone, including Nick, turned to look at her. A second later the edge of the folder burst into flames.

chapter

2

"Now you've done it!" cried Diane, her face white with fear. She jumped up, knocking her chair to the floor. "You've really done it!"

She turned and ran from the room.

For a moment nobody moved. Then Andrea grabbed the folder from Nick and shook it till the flames died out.

"What's with your friend?" asked Max. "Why did she go bananas?"

"She's your friend too," said Jill. "You know, playing with lighters in the library isn't exactly the swiftest thing you've ever done."

"It's a good thing Miss Dotson isn't here," added Andrea. "I'm going to go see if Diane's all right."

"I'll go with you," said Jill. "See you guys in geography."

As they walked out into the hall, Andrea dropped the blackened folder into the overflowing trash can by the door.

They found Diane standing by an open window, breathing deeply, her whole body trembling.

Jill put an arm around her. "Hey, Diane," she said gently. "What is it?"

Diane turned her stricken face to the other girls. "I *hate* fire," she said. "I just *hate* it."

"It's okay," said Andrea. "But don't you think you're overreacting just the teensiest bit? No one was hurt. Nothing got burned but a crummy folder."

"I guess you're right," said Diane. "Sorry. I'm all right now."

But Jill saw that she still looked frightened—almost haunted.

A few minutes later Jill sat in algebra class trying to answer some sample problems. "If a train starts out from Chicago at fifty miles an hour," one problem began, "and another train starts at the same time from San Francisco at sixty-five miles an hour . . ."

Why would they do that? Jill thought. Who takes the train these days?

It was no use. She just couldn't concentrate on the stupid trains. Her eyes kept turning to the window, where pink and creamy white dogwood trees were blossoming, and her mind kept going back to the library and the strange way that Diane had reacted to the fire.

Diane was what Jill's mother called "high-strung." Maybe it will be good for her to have an old friend around, thought Jill.

And maybe it'll be good for *me,* she thought. This Gabe really sounded interesting. She'd never known a guy who was really into music. Nick and Max were all right. But she couldn't take them seriously as anything more than friends.

She tried to imagine Gabe's green eyes as Diane had described them, and then, suddenly, she smelled something pungent and sour.

Smoke.

As she watched, the dogwoods were partially obscured by thick, black smoke. Jill felt her heart tighten in her chest.

An instant later the fire alarm began to ring.

An instant after *that* the school intercom crackled and the principal's voice came on, faint against the wail of the alarm.

"All fire monitors to their stations," he said.

His next words were drowned out by a shriek. "This is real!" a girl screamed in a panicky voice.

"Just stay calm," said Mr. Molitor, the math teacher. His voice was low and steady, but Jill thought he looked scared. "There's plenty of time to get out. Line up by the door."

Her heart still thudding, Jill grabbed her backpack and stood up, then joined the line and followed the teacher out into the smoky second floor hall and down the stairs to the nearest exit.

The air filled with the wail of sirens. By the time Jill's class had reached the courtyard, fire fighters in heavy black raincoats and hats were swarming into the building.

Jill searched for Diane and Andrea, but they both had classes on the other side of the school. I'll bet Diane's really freaking out, Jill thought. If she was scared of a couple of lighters in the library . . .

The library.

Terry Ryan, one of the boys in her class, nudged her just then. "Look!" he said. "The fire's in the library!"

Jill raised her eyes to where he was pointing and saw the smoke billowing out the second floor windows beside the library stacks. Immediately she realized what must have happened.

Two fire fighters, their faces dark with soot, were coming outside now, dragging a large, blackened trash basket. The contents of the basket had been doused with water, but tendrils of smoke still curled up from the charred mess.

It was the library trash can.

The one Andrea had dropped the burnt folder into.

chapter

3

"**H**ey, I didn't know it was still on fire," said Andrea. She sucked the rest of her root beer through a striped straw, then reached for a french fry from the double-order sitting in front of Nick. "Yuck, these are so salty! Hey, Nick, you ever consider just eating directly from the salt shaker?"

"If you don't like them, order your own," said Nick, pulling the plate away from her. "Besides, I thought you were on a diet." He always ordered doubles of everything but stayed as skinny as a stick.

"I've got to keep my strength up," cracked Andrea. "In case they arrest me for burning the school down."

"Lighten up, Andrea," said Max. "No one knows it was your fault."

"It was Nick's fault anyway," added Jill. "And Max's. Admit it, guys, you planned the whole thing so we wouldn't have the geography quiz."

"It worked too," said Max.

"Well, maybe you can do it again next week so I

won't have to turn in my research paper," said Jill. "That's Wednesday at nine-forty."

"I couldn't believe all that smoke," said Andrea. "Just from one little wastebasket fire."

"Fires are so frightening," said Diane in a small voice. It was the first time she had spoken, except to order a Coke, since the five friends had gone into Pete's Pizza.

"What's your problem?" asked Max. "No one was hurt. There was no damage."

"There could have been," said Diane. She shuddered.

"You know," said Jill, "Diane's right. Fire *can* be a very scary—"

"Look!" said Diane suddenly, cutting her off. "Look who's here!"

Jill glanced up, half expecting to see the fire chief. The door had just swung open, and a tall, muscular boy stood framed in it against the setting sun. He was dressed in faded 501 jeans and a gray rugby shirt. His thick, sandy hair curled above a broad, handsome face.

"Gabe! Over here!" Diane wriggled out of the booth and ran over to give him a big, friendly hug.

"Who's the new dude?" asked Max.

"Obviously a friend of Diane's," said Nick.

"She wasn't kidding," Andrea whispered to Jill, checking out the new arrival. "That guy is *gorgeous.*"

Diane came back to the booth, leading Gabe by the arm. "This is my good friend Gabe Miller," she said, beaming. Her face had turned from serious to sparkling, and Jill was aware again of how pretty Diane was when she smiled.

Smiling herself, she felt a little shiver pass through her as her eyes met Gabe's.

He was the handsomest boy she had ever seen outside the movies, and his eyes were just as green as Diane had described—a clear bottle green, with a sparkling intensity almost like fire.

Gabe held her gaze a moment longer, then turned to each of the others, an ironic half smile on his lips. "How you doing," he said as Diane introduced each in turn.

Why did Jill have the feeling that Gabe didn't really want to be there?

"Hey—here's a chair," said Max. He pulled one over from an empty table.

Gabe turned the chair around so that its back was against the table; then he straddled it, facing the others. "Thanks," he said without glancing at Max. Instead he kept staring first at Andrea, then back at Jill, a slow secret smile on his face. "So this is where it's all happening," he said sarcastically.

"Come on, Gabe," said Diane. "Shadyside is okay. You're going to like it here. I promise."

"I don't know about that," said Gabe with a shrug.

"Diane said you're from Center City," said Andrea.

"Yeah?" said Gabe. "What else did she tell you about me?"

"She said you're into music," said Jill. "That you write your own songs."

"I fool around a little," said Gabe with the same strange smile.

"Really?" said Nick. "Maybe you could help me with the guitar."

"Oh, get real, Nick," said Andrea. "You only know two chords."

14

"Well, that's why I need help," said Nick. "You play guitar, Gabe?"

"It's one of my instruments," said Gabe.

"What're the other ones?" asked Max.

"I play lots of instruments," said Gabe, appearing to lose interest in the conversation.

"For heaven's sake, Max," said Andrea. "Gabe just got here. Give him a break."

"What I want to know is how come you're here now," Diane said to Gabe. "I thought you and your mom weren't coming till next week."

"Yeah, well, the people who bought our house wanted to move in early, so here I am."

"Not as exciting here as in the city, I guess," said Max.

"It's different," said Gabe.

"Actually, we had quite a bit of excitement today," said Jill. She found herself wanting to defend Shadyside, for no reason she could think of.

"Yeah?" said Gabe, gazing at Jill with interest.

"What Jill means," said Andrea, "is that we had a fire at school. It was really no big deal."

"Hey," said Nick. "I call it a pretty big deal since we got geography canceled."

"You mean you started the fire?" said Gabe. He sounded more interested.

"Well, sort of," said Max. "Nick set a folder on fire. It was just a goof. And Andrea tossed it in a wastebasket before the fire was out."

"That's it?" said Gabe. "You set a wastebasket fire?"

"Well, yeah," said Nick.

"And the fire trucks came and everything?"

"Yeah, they did," said Nick. "It was awesome."

For a long moment Gabe didn't answer; then he shook his head. "So what you're telling me," he said to Max, "is that the most exciting thing that's happened around here is a wastebasket fire that was an accident?"

"We told you it was no big deal," said Andrea. "But it was a little exciting."

"You know," Gabe went on, almost to himself, "it takes guts to set a fire deliberately."

"Yeah?" said Max. "You ever set one?"

Gabe didn't reply, just shrugged, a strange smile on his face, his green eyes staring into the distance.

Jill stared at him, confused. What is he talking about? she wondered. Does he set fires deliberately? She stared at her friends, startled by the excitement on their faces.

Then she turned to Diane. Diane had her serious face on again. She was staring at Gabe, slowly shaking her head as if sending him a message.

What's going on? Jill wondered. Does Diane know more about Gabe than she wants us to know?

chapter
4

"*H*appy pizza day!" said Nick, carefully setting his overloaded tray down on the lunchroom table.

"Whoa!" exclaimed Jill. "Nick, you have *six* slices there!"

"It was all I could afford," Nick cracked. He opened his mouth and began to shovel in pizza.

Max, sitting next to Nick and across from Jill, was staring down at a big salad, while the three girls and Nick ate pizza.

"I'm so glad it's Friday," said Jill. "And not just because it's pizza day in the cafeteria."

"I second that!" said Andrea. She turned to Max. "What's your problem? You usually have as many slices as Nick."

"I'm just not too hungry today," said Max, picking at his salad.

"He's trying to lose weight," said Nick. "To look more like Gabe."

"Lay off!" said Max, his ruddy face flushing even

17

redder. "There's nothing wrong with trying to take care of yourself a little."

"If you want to look like Gabe, it's going to take a lot more than a salad," said Andrea.

"Well, I think it's just fine if Max wants to try to lose some weight," said Diane. "Good for you." Diane was always coming to the rescue of anyone who got teased too much.

"Speaking of Gabe," Andrea went on, ignoring her, "I haven't seen him all day. Is he in school?"

"His parents' furniture was supposed to be delivered today," said Diane. "Maybe he stayed home to— Oh, there he is now." She stood up and waved so that Gabe would see her.

Gabe ambled over to the table and sat down next to Jill, favoring her with his slow smile. Jill felt flustered and unsure of what to say.

"I was just in the gym doing some extra crunches and chins," Gabe said. "You know, the phys. ed. program here is pathetic. They must be trying to turn out couch potatoes."

"That's not true," said Nick. "We've got one of the best swimming programs in the state."

"Not to mention a great gymnastics program," said Jill. "You know, Andrea's going to be All-State this year."

"Is that right?" said Gabe. He gave Andrea an appreciative glance.

"Well, I don't know if I'll actually get to the championship," said Andrea. "But that reminds me. I've been meaning to ask you—"

"Let's not talk about that now," Diane interrupted. "Gabe, did your parents' stuff get delivered okay?"

"Yeah, the movers came first thing yesterday morning," said Gabe. "So I guess that means I'm stuck here in good old Shadyside."

"Oh, come on," said Jill, suddenly exasperated. "You haven't been here long enough to give Shadyside a chance."

"I've been here long enough to know the pizza's terrible," Gabe said, dropping a half-eaten piece onto his tray.

"What do you expect?" said Diane. "This is the school cafeteria. You ought to try the pizza at Pete's."

"I ordered in from there the other night," said Gabe. "Definitely second-rate."

"Well, all right, maybe the pizza doesn't live up to your big-city standards, but Shadyside has a lot of good things," said Nick.

"Like what?"

"Well, Dobie's has the best ice cream I've ever tasted," said Jill. "I bet even you would agree it's— excuse the expression—first-rate."

"Well, at least I won't starve here," said Gabe. "Just probably die of boredom."

"There's lots of stuff to do here too," Jill went on, wondering why she was spending so much effort on defending Shadyside. "We've got Red Heat, a great dance club, and the bowling alley, and— Well, okay, you've probably got things like that in Center City, but I'll bet you don't have as many outdoor places as we do."

"Wow! I don't know if I can take all the excitement," cracked Gabe.

"Oh, Gabe," said Diane and sighed. "Can't you even try to like it here? If you just gave it a chance, I know you'd be happy."

"Hey, I'll try," said Gabe. "But it's not easy. Can

you name one thing that Shadyside has that Center City doesn't?"

"We have a haunted street," said Max.

"You have a what?"

"Fear Street," said Jill with a little shiver. "But that's not exactly one of the great things about Shadyside."

"Fear Street? You have a street called Fear Street?"

"It was named after Simon Fear, one of the first settlers here," Max added. "You can still see the ruins of his mansion. Some of the houses on the street are supposed to be haunted."

"What is it?" asked Gabe. "Some sort of theme park?"

"No," said Andrea, for once sounding serious. "It's not a joke. At the end of the street there's a creepy old cemetery surrounded by woods. Weird things have happened around Fear Street. People have disappeared there, and there've been a number of unsolved murders."

"Fear Street sounds interesting," said Gabe. "I'd like to see it."

"How about this weekend?" said Diane suddenly. "My parents just bought a cabin on the lake in the Fear Street woods. It's really beautiful out there."

"Your parents bought a haunted cabin?" asked Gabe.

"Of course not!" said Diane. "The woods are sort of creepy, but the cabin's cool. Let's do it! We could all go for a picnic."

"Nah," said Gabe. "I'd like to, Di, but I promised my folks I'd help them unpack this weekend."

"The whole weekend?" asked Andrea.

"I think so," said Gabe.

20

"Too bad we can't just get this afternoon off," said Max.

"Right," said Jill. "'I'm sorry, Mr. Molitor, I can't come to algebra because I have an emergency picnic to go to.'"

"Hey," said Gabe. "What if there really was an emergency?"

"What do you mean?" asked Jill.

"Well, remember what you told me last week, about starting a wastebasket fire? And how it got you out of a geography quiz?"

"That was just an accident," said Jill. She had a feeling she didn't want to hear what else Gabe had to say.

"Yeah, well, what if we set a *real* fire? One that's bad enough to cancel classes?" Gabe said it as casually as if he'd suggested going back for seconds on lunch.

"Oh, right," said Max. "Or why don't we call in a bomb threat to the principal?"

"Or—wait—I've got it," cracked Andrea. "Why don't we *kidnap* the principal?"

"Right," agreed Nick. "And bring him along on the picnic. He'd probably like the afternoon off too."

By now everyone was laughing.

"They're all good ideas," said Gabe, "but I vote for the fire."

"Me too," said Max. "We already know that works."

"Yeah, but who's going to set it?" said Andrea.

"Someone with guts," said Gabe. He was smiling a mocking smile, and Jill suddenly thought that he might be serious.

"Are you serious?" blurted out Max as if reading Jill's thoughts.

Gabe shrugged. "Didn't you just say you'd like to take the afternoon off?"

"Well, yeah, but I didn't mean—"

"Didn't mean what?" said Gabe. "Would you like the afternoon off or not?"

"Well, sure I would. But—are you saying we should set a real fire?" Max looked dumbfounded.

"Not we," said Gabe. "You."

"Me?" Max's voice suddenly squeaked. "Why me?"

"Or Nick," said Gabe casually. "Of course, if no one has the guts, we can just forget the whole thing."

"Are you crazy?" exclaimed Nick. "We could get kicked out of school—for good!"

"Gabe, you can't be serious!" Jill cried.

"You'd better not be," said Diane. Jill thought she was pleading with Gabe with her eyes. "I don't want to hear any more talk about fires," Diane said suddenly. "I—I have to go study for geography class." She stood up abruptly and walked off.

"Diane—" Jill called after her.

"Don't worry about Diane," said Gabe. "She's always been a little jumpy." He turned to Andrea. "What do you think about the idea, Andrea?"

Andrea smiled excitedly. "I'm just waiting to see if anyone will really do it."

"Probably not," said Gabe. "This is Shadyside, land of the wimp."

He casually pulled a disposable lighter out of his pocket and put it on the table. "It wouldn't be hard, you know," he said. "I've been keeping an eye on the boys' room. Nobody's gone in there for fifteen minutes."

For a moment nobody said anything. They all stared at the lighter as if it were a bomb.

Then suddenly Max reached out and grabbed it.

"Max," said Jill, suddenly nervous. "You don't have to do anything you don't want to."

Max didn't answer. He seemed to make a sudden decision, jumped up, and walked into the boys' room.

Jill, Andrea, Nick, and Gabe all stared after him.

"He's not really going to set a fire," said Jill, hoping he wouldn't.

"I don't know," said Gabe. "He seemed pretty determined to me."

"He probably just had to go," said Andrea. "I've known Max for three years, and he just doesn't—"

Her words were cut off by the bell ending lunch hour and the usual mad scramble as kids hurried to dump their trays and head for class.

Jill was just picking up her tray when she heard a sudden whooshing noise, then a loud explosion, and the door to the boys' restroom blew off its hinges. An instant later bright orange flames shot into the cafeteria.

chapter

5

*E*veryone's acting like it's a big joke, Jill thought. And actually, in a way, it was.

Nick, wearing cutoff jeans and a huge, goofy-looking straw hat, was unpacking picnic things from the back of his father's old station wagon and tossing them, one at a time, to Andrea and Gabe, who were both whooping and laughing.

Jill and Andrea were both dressed in short beach dresses over their new bathing suits, while Gabe was wearing black spandex bicycle shorts and a cutoff T-shirt that made him look like a finalist in the Mr. America contest. Even Max was wearing swimming trunks, his pudgy body overlapping the waistband only slightly.

Diane was the only one not wearing a bathing suit. She had on jeans and a long-sleeved T-shirt with flowers printed on it. "I have an allergy to the sun," she reminded them. "But that doesn't mean the rest of you can't go in the water." While the others continued

24

to unload the car, she helped set things up on the long redwood table.

Jill had never seen her friends so excited. But then, they had never come close to burning down the school before.

She still wasn't sure how she felt about it. When the flames had erupted into the cafeteria, Jill had been more frightened than ever before in her life. Her knees shaking, she had followed the others out the door through screams and thick, choking smoke.

Max! she kept thinking. He was *in there* when it exploded.

Then a moment later Max appeared from the side door behind the cafeteria.

"Max!" she cried. "Are you all right? We weren't sure if you got out!"

Before he could answer, Diane had come running up to them as they stood in a knot in the middle of the soccer field.

"What happened?" she demanded, her face pale.

"We did it, that's what!" said Andrea with an exultant whoop. "Or rather, Max did it. . . ."

"Hey, quiet!" Max said in a strangled voice. He looked pale and shaken.

"What a boom!" exulted Gabe. "But how did you manage to—"

"I don't want to talk about it here!" said Max.

"Nobody can hear us," said Andrea. "Wow, do you believe this?"

Once again fire trucks roared into the school grounds, their sirens blaring. This time the fire fighters hooked up their hoses and charged into the building with water streaming in front of them.

Cars honked loudly, loudspeakers squawked, and there were excited shouts and cries. It was so noisy Jill could hardly think. She just turned with the others and silently watched.

"I'm really glad I wasn't in the cafeteria," Diane told Jill. "It must have been really scary."

"It was," Jill agreed.

"Are you guys sure I can't get caught?" Max asked nervously.

"Relax!" said Gabe, exasperated. "There's no way anyone can know. No one was in the rest room, and there were a million people coming and going."

"I didn't know it would be such a big fire," Max went on. "I never meant to do so much damage."

"So the rest room will be closed for a few days," said Andrea. "Big deal."

"There was this big can of cleaning solution right next to the wastebasket," said Max. "That's what must have exploded. I lit some papers in the wastebasket and ran. I was lucky. The can exploded just seconds after I got out. What a sound!"

"That was what made it such an awesome fire," said Gabe.

"Don't worry, Max," said Diane sympathetically. "You got carried away by Gabe's dare. I know you didn't mean to do it."

Later, after the fire was out, the fire marshal had come and questioned some kids who had been in the cafeteria. But no one had seen anything unusual. Because of the smoke damage, school had been canceled for the rest of the day.

"All the stuff is out of the car," Max announced. "Now let's eat."

"We've got to let the coals burn down in the grill," said Diane. "Why don't you guys go for a swim?"

"First I want to see Diane's haunted cabin," said Gabe. "Come on, Diane, let us in."

"My parents haven't finished fixing it up yet," said Diane. "But I guess we could look inside."

From the outside it looked like a rustic old cabin, but on the inside it was startlingly modern. Diane's parents were renovating it, and the furniture was all chic and sleek looking. Artwork—mobiles, paintings, and metal sculptures in progress—hung everywhere in the single big room. Diane's father had a workbench set up with his blowtorch and cutting tools. "My dad plans to use this as his studio on weekends," Diane explained. "He likes the light out here." Her father taught metal sculpture at the junior college, and his work had won several local awards.

"I never did understand your father's sculptures," Gabe told Diane. "But this place is great! Too bad it's not really haunted."

"Haven't you had enough excitement for one day?" asked Andrea, laughing.

"Me?" said Gabe. "No way! Come on, let's go check out the lake!"

The water was icy, a frigid contrast to the warm early-spring air, and Jill gave up after a few minutes and joined Diane on the dock. Her arms were covered with goosebumps as she slipped on her beach dress.

In the center of the lake Nick and Max were clowning around, pushing each other off the float. Off to the side, Gabe and Andrea were treading water, talking animatedly. Then Max materialized next to them. There was some shouting and splashing, and then Andrea swam back to the shore. She got out of the water, shivering, and sat beside her friends.

"I can't believe this," Andrea said. "Max started telling Gabe what a good swimmer Nick is, so now they're going to have a race. They're going to swim from the float to here and back, and we're supposed to watch to make sure both of them touch the dock."

"Gabe's a good athlete," said Diane. "But I don't know if he can swim as well as Nick."

"My money's on Nick," said Jill.

"Really?" said Andrea. "It's a bet! If Nick wins, I'll let you borrow my red leather jacket whenever you want. And if Gabe wins, you have to do my history homework all next week."

"It's a bet," said Jill, laughing.

The three boys were now standing on the float. Max raised his hand, and the girls could hear him call out, "On your mark, get set, *go!*"

Nick and Gabe dived into the water and began swimming for the dock with smooth, clean strokes. Jill watched as they streaked through the water. "Come on, Nick!" she shouted.

"Go, Gabe!" yelled Andrea.

"Go, go, go!" screamed Diane. Jill didn't know who Diane was rooting for, but no matter who won, they were all having fun watching.

When the boys reached the dock, Nick was ahead of Gabe, and as they raced back to the float, his lead widened. "Go, Nick, go!" Jill yelled. Then, just before they reached the float, Nick slowed down and Gabe won by a head.

Andrea stood and cheered loudly, then sat back down. "Wow!" she said. "Is there anything Gabe can't do?"

"What were you guys talking about out there?" Diane asked.

"Remember your idea that Gabe could write some music for my floor routine?" said Andrea. "Well, I asked him about it, and he said he's interested. He's going to watch me practice to get some ideas."

"That's great," said Jill.

"Maybe it will make him feel more involved in things," said Diane. But she didn't sound as happy about it as Jill had thought she would—especially since it had been her idea in the first place.

"I wouldn't mind getting him a *lot* more involved," said Andrea, her eyes on the boys as they swam lazily toward the shore. "Diane, can I ask you something personal?"

"Sure," said Diane.

"I just want to know . . . I mean, well, would you have any objections if I went out with Gabe?"

Jill turned to Diane with interest. She had been wondering the same thing.

For a moment Diane didn't answer; then she shrugged. "Why would I have any objections?" she asked. Then she quickly added, "But he isn't really your type."

"Don't be too sure about that," said Andrea. "I just wanted to make sure that there isn't anything between you and Gabe before I—"

"We're just friends," said Diane.

"And that's all?"

"That's all," Diane repeated. "Gabe's an old family friend." Jill couldn't see Diane's face, but the whole conversation was making Diane feel uncomfortable. Jill was trying to figure out why when she was suddenly splashed from head to foot by the boys.

"Hey—watch out!" she shouted, leaping up.

"What's for supper?" asked Max. "We're starved."

"That was a terrific race," said Diane. "You were both great. It was like watching the Olympics."

"You have a great stroke," said Andrea, staring boldly at Gabe.

"What happened, Nick?" asked Jill. "I thought for sure you were winning."

"Oh, I got a cramp and had to slow down."

"Excuses, excuses," said Gabe.

"Well, that's what happened," said Nick. He flashed Gabe an angry look.

"Hey, I was just kidding," said Gabe. "Terrific race. I mean it." He clapped Nick on the shoulder and offered his hand. Nick took it, but Jill knew Nick was still unhappy.

After the six teens stuffed themselves on hot dogs and salad, Diane went into the cabin and brought out a battered old guitar. "Remember this, Gabe?" she asked.

"My first guitar!" he said, laughing. "I can't believe you still have it."

"Gabe gave this to me a long time ago when I was sick," Diane said. "I never learned to play it, but my father likes it. Play something for us, please?"

"Oh, I don't know," said Gabe.

"Yeah, come on, Gabe," Nick chimed in. "Let's hear you play."

Gabe shrugged and began to tune the strings. It was getting dark, and Diane and Andrea set candles around the patio area, adding a warm glow to the deepening dusk.

Gabe finished tuning up and began to strum the

guitar, and immediately everyone fell silent. Somehow he made real music come out of that battered old guitar. Then he began to sing in a husky baritone. He's really good, Jill thought. Maybe Andrea's right. Maybe Gabe really can do anything.

The candles were cheery looking as the trees became black, lacy silhouettes against a pale purple sky. Gabe started playing some old favorites, and they all sang. Jill felt more contented than she had in a long time. This is great, she thought—just hanging out with my best friends, singing, relaxing. Things had really changed since Gabe had come to Shadyside, and she decided they had changed for the better. He was shaking them out of their old patterns, getting them to try new things, even if some of them were sort of wild.

After a while Gabe put the guitar down and stretched. "That's enough for now," he said. "I'm a little out of practice."

"I thought you sounded great," said Andrea.

"Hey," said Nick, suddenly reading his watch. "I've got to get the car home."

Diane took the guitar back inside and locked up the cabin. "We've got to pick up every solitary scrap or my parents will have a fit," she told the others. "And make sure the fire's completely out."

"Don't give that job to Andrea," cracked Nick. "Remember what happened last week."

"Or Max," added Jill. "The firebug of Shadyside High."

"Very funny," said Max. "Thanks for reminding me. The cops are probably at my house now."

"Oh, quit worrying," said Andrea.

"What's so bad about a little fire?" added Gabe.

He picked up one of the candles from the picnic table. Jill thought he was going to blow it out. But then she and the others watched in horror and fascination as he brought his other hand down close to the flame—and held it there. As the flame licked at his hand, the expression on his face didn't change.

chapter

6

"What do you think, guys?" asked Diane. "Ready to shop till we drop?" She was gazing eagerly outside the snack bar at the Division Street Mall.

"Not me," said Jill. "I already spent my entire clothes allowance for the year!"

"Bummer," said Diane. "I have my mom's charge card. She says I need some new clothes."

"I wish my mom would say that," said Andrea. "My mom always goes, 'Oh, no, you don't need that. You already have too many things in your closet!'"

"Well, I'm stuffed," said Diane. "Let's get out of here."

"Good idea." Jill finished her sundae and wiped her face. "I'll bet that had a hundred million calories in it."

"What do you care?" said Andrea. "You're not on a diet."

"Yeah, well, if I'm going to stay *off* one, we'd better

get some exercise. Anyone want to check out the upper level?"

"Sure," said Andrea. "Maybe we'll run into the guys."

"Haven't you had enough of them in school?"

"Well," Andrea replied, "I thought maybe I could talk to Gabe about the music he's going to do for my program."

"Oh, yeah?" said Jill. "How's that going?"

"Well, we haven't actually gotten anything together yet. He hasn't been able to come to my practice."

The girls paid for their desserts and left the Olde Sweete Shoppe. It was Tuesday Sale Night, and the mall was jammed with bargain hunters.

"Wow, it's really crowded," said Jill. "Even if the boys are here, we wouldn't be able to find them."

"I don't think Gabe hangs out in malls," Diane said.

"You're probably right," said Andrea. "He's much too cool for that."

The first shop at the top of the stairs was the Shadyside Pet Shop, and Diane always had to check out the dogs and cats. She wasn't allowed to have a pet of her own because her father was allergic.

"Oh, look at that one, Jill," Diane said, pointing to a white kitten. "It looks just like Mittsy."

Jill laughed. The little cat did look like Mittsy, Jill's golden-eyed Persian. In a nearby window two very fluffy terrier puppies were playing with each other, rolling over and over in the shredded paper. Jill and Diane stood with their noses against the glass, oohing and aahing.

"Will you guys hurry up?" asked Andrea. "The mall closes in half an hour."

"Oh, come on, Andrea," said Diane. "Just 'cause you don't like animals . . ."

"I like them okay," said Andrea impatiently. "I just never understand why people make idiots of themselves over them. I'm more interested in animals of another sort—boy animals."

"Especially one," teased Jill.

"Did you ever see such green eyes?" Andrea exclaimed.

Jill glanced at the puppies in the window, then realized Andrea was talking about Gabe.

"You were absolutely right about his eyes, Diane," Andrea said. Diane didn't answer. "How did you meet him, anyway?"

"We lived next door to each other when we were little," said Diane. "We went to kindergarten together."

"Was he always so wild?"

"Well," said Diane, "Gabe was always getting in trouble, if that's what you mean. His mother always said I was a good influence on him." She smiled as she remembered. "I could never stop him from anything he really wanted to do, though."

"I have a feeling nobody could stop Gabe if he was after something," said Andrea. "He's a guy who seems to know exactly what he wants."

"That's right," said Diane. "That's exactly right." She spoke very seriously, and once again Jill had the feeling that Diane was keeping something secret about Gabe.

The girls continued to walk along the upper level, checking out all the windows. The Athlete's Den had a big display of weight-lifting equipment. "Gabe told me he lifts weights," Andrea said. "How long has he been doing that, Diane?"

"Probably since kindergarten," said Jill. "Honestly, Andrea, what do you think Diane is—Gabe's keeper?"

"I don't mind," said Diane. "After all, I know Gabe better than anyone." She was silent a moment, then went on. "He was always interested in sports," she told Andrea. "I think he started lifting weights a couple years ago."

"Oh, yeah?" said Andrea. "What sports did he play?"

Diane sighed. "I don't remember everything. He was in Little League baseball, and in middle school he played soccer and basketball."

"I'll bet he was good at them, wasn't he?"

"I guess he's a natural athlete," said Diane.

"When he and Nick were in that race," Andrea went on, "I couldn't believe how fast he was. I mean, Nick's a really good swimmer, and for Gabe to have beaten him . . ."

"Don't forget Nick got a cramp," said Jill.

"So he says," said Andrea. "It sounded like an excuse to me. Anyway, why are you defending Nick? Aren't you the least bit interested in Gabe too?"

Jill didn't answer for a moment. The problem was that she *was* interested in Gabe—very interested— but she was bothered by him too. There was something about him—and her feelings for him—that made her very uncomfortable. "I just thought it was weird when he stuck his hand in the candle flame," she said at last.

"That was the coolest thing of all," said Andrea. "I never saw anyone do anything like that before. I couldn't believe it!" She laughed. "And did you see the looks on the other guys' faces when he did it? I thought they were both going to die of jealousy."

"I was afraid Max was going to try it next," said Jill.

"Me too," said Andrea. "Hey, Diane, have you ever seen Gabe do anything like that before?"

Diane shrugged. "Not exactly like that," she said. Instead of explaining what she meant, she abruptly started to cross to the other side of the wide walkway. "I want to go into Benniger's for a minute. I need a new shirt."

Jill and Andrea followed her across the walkway to the large specialty shop. Signs hung in every window: Spring Madness Sale and All Merchandise Slashed Forty Percent.

"You don't want to go in here, Diane," cracked Andrea. "All the merchandise is slashed."

"Very funny," said Diane. "I won't take long."

With a little smile, she headed for the sportswear racks. Jill had the feeling that Diane was tired of talking about Gabe or at least of answering questions about him. While Diane looked at tops, Jill fingered through the silk scarves. Her mother's birthday was coming up and she was looking for an inspiration. But instead of concentrating on the scarves, she kept thinking back to the picnic, to everything that had happened with Gabe, from when he had goaded Max into setting the fire until he had put his hand in the candle flame. It must have hurt, she thought. What had he been trying to prove? And who had he been trying to prove it to?

As she idly looked through the scarves, she found one in bright shades of purple and pink, her mother's colors. She turned to show it to the other girls, but they were nowhere in sight. Probably trying on clothes, she thought. She held on to the purple scarf and began looking through the rest.

Suddenly a piercing shriek filled the store. "No!" A voice screamed in panic and terror, "Go away! Leave me alone!"

Jill froze, her heart pounding.

The anguished voice was Diane's.

chapter
7

Dropping the purple scarf, Jill ran as quickly as she could to the back of the store, then through the curtains that hid the dressing room area. Turning the corner, she literally bumped into Andrea. "Whoa!" she said. "Sorry! Did you hear—"

"I couldn't miss it," said Andrea. "I was the one she was yelling at."

"What?" Jill looked at her friend in confusion. "Is Diane all right? What's going on?"

"Ask her yourself," said Andrea, shrugging. "All I know is I was going to try this on"—she held up a lime-green T-shirt—"so I went into what I thought was an empty dressing room. Only it turned out Diane was in it."

"Well, did she think you were trying to break in on her, or what?"

"I don't know," said Andrea. "She just went berserk. And she wasn't even undressed; she was just unbuttoning one of the shirts."

Jill frowned. "Well, you know how modest she is," she said after a moment. "I mean, she always dresses in the stalls in phys. ed."

"Sure, I know that," said Andrea. "But this is crazy!"

"Maybe I'd better look in and see if she's all right," said Jill.

"If I were you I'd leave her alone till she's through in there," said Andrea. "Anyway, I still want to try on this T-shirt. Hold my purse, will you?"

She stepped into one of the booths while Jill waited in the corridor. What in the world could be wrong with Diane? she wondered.

Andrea returned—without the T-shirt. "No luck," she reported.

Jill scarcely heard her. Why is Diane taking so long? she asked herself. Maybe I should just go in there and find out—

But at that moment Diane came out of the dressing room, holding several blouses on hangers. As soon as she spotted her friends, she smiled sheepishly.

"I'm sorry about before, Andrea," she said. "I just didn't recognize you when you came in the dressing room."

"Didn't recognize me?" said Andrea in disbelief. "Who'd you think I was? Freddy Kreuger?"

"I was thinking about something else," Diane said. "I wasn't expecting anyone to come in."

"Well, no problem," said Jill. But she wasn't sure about it. Diane still looked upset, and despite her sarcasm, Andrea seemed bothered by the incident.

Jill remembered the sound of Diane's scream—the sheer terror in it.

Andrea must have done—or said—something to have frightened Diane so badly, whether she realized it or not.

But what?

Pulling into her driveway, Jill realized that she had forgotten to buy the purple scarf in all the excitement. And her mother's birthday was in just a few days. Her mom said she had everything she wanted, but Jill still wanted to get her something special.

Maybe if she hung out with her parents for a while, she'd get some other ideas.

She went into the kitchen and poured a glass of ginger ale, then followed the sounds of the television to the family room. Her parents were sitting on the sofa, watching the tube, while Mittsy sat on the ottoman grooming her long, shiny fur.

Jill smiled to herself when she saw that her parents were holding hands. Whenever they did that, she was a little embarrassed, but she also thought it was kind of sweet. They'd been married for over twenty years and still did that kind of stuff. "Hi," she said.

"Hi, dear," said her mother. "How was shopping?"

"Okay," she said. "You'll be happy to hear I didn't buy anything."

Jill sat on the ottoman and picked up Mittsy.

"We're watching a nature show," said her father. "It's about the attempts being made to save the Amazon forest. Mittsy seemed to be interested."

"Is that right, Mitts?" said Jill. She raised her eyes then to check out the show. Thick green foliage filled the screen, along with the droning voice of an earnest-sounding announcer. "Oh, look, Mittsy," she told her pet. "There's one of your little cousins. It's an ocelot. See?" Mittsy wriggled as Jill attempted to turn the cat's head toward the screen.

"Persians," Jill said in mock disgust. "They have no interest in culture."

"Hal called while you were gone," Jill's mother said. "He's thinking of bringing a girlfriend home for spring vacation."

"Really?" said Jill. Hal was her older brother, and he'd been away at college for three years. Most of the time she didn't miss him, but she wasn't sure she liked the idea of his bringing a girl around. That sounded serious.

"He wanted to know how you're doing," added her father. "We told him about the good grades you've been getting."

"I'm sure he was just dying to hear that," said Jill. "But that reminds me, I want to go over my research paper for tomorrow. Good night," she added, kissing both her parents on the cheek.

Jill had finished everything she had to do on the paper that afternoon, but for some reason she felt like being alone for a while. The trip to the mall had been strangely troubling.

First, Andrea had kept going on and on about Gabe, and then that weird thing had happened in the dressing room between Diane and Andrea. Maybe it's just spring fever, she thought.

She put her term paper and books into her day pack, then changed into her nightgown and washed her face. She was just weaving her long hair into a single braid when the phone rang.

"Hello?" She glanced at the clock by her bed. It was almost eleven o'clock.

"Jill?" said a familiar voice she couldn't quite place. "I hope it's not too late to call."

"I was just getting ready for bed," she said, annoyed. "Who is this?"

"It's Gabe."

For a moment she couldn't answer. For some reason her heart had started beating really fast.

"Jill? Are you there?"

"I'm here," she said. "Hi, Gabe." Then, as casually as she could say it, she added, "What's up?"

"Nothing much," he said. "I've been really busy for the past couple of days and haven't seen you much. What've you been doing?"

"The usual stuff," she said. "You know. School, gymnastics, shopping. But you knew that. You were at lunch today when Andrea and Diane and I made plans to go to the mall."

"I guess I wasn't paying attention," said Gabe. "Besides, I wanted to talk to you in private."

"What about?" she asked.

"Oh, things," he said. She imagined she could see his mocking smile.

"What kind of things?"

"Well, for instance," he said, "Shadyside things. You know you're always telling me what a great place Shadyside is."

"Well, it is. So?"

"So I was thinking maybe you'd like to show me some of those great things. Up close and personal."

"Well, sure," said Jill, confused. "Any time. Whatever you want to see. We can borrow Nick's father's car and go—"

"Not with the other kids," he said. "You and me. Me and you. Get it?"

"Oh," said Jill. She suddenly realized that he was asking her out.

"So what about this weekend?" he asked. "Saturday night?"

"Well, uh—I'll have to check," said Jill.

"What's the matter? Afraid I'll do something crazy?"

Jill was too surprised to answer. The truth was she *was* a little afraid of what he might do.

Gabe laughed. "Don't worry. I never do anything without a good reason."

"What do you mean?" said Jill, totally confused.

"Never mind," said Gabe, sounding more serious. "The things you don't know can't hurt you. Now what about Saturday night? Or would Friday be better?"

"Saturday's fine," Jill said, making a sudden decision.

"Really? Great," he said. "You be thinking about the best things to do in Shadyside on a Saturday night. I'll pick you up at seven."

Gabe's voice sounded in her mind long after she hung up the phone. A part of her was excited by the thought of going out with him. She had felt attracted to him from the first time she'd seen him.

But another part was nervous. For one thing, Andrea was making no secret about how she felt about Gabe. What would Andrea say if she found out?

For another thing, Gabe was so unpredictable.

What had he meant when he said he never did anything without a reason? Or that what Jill didn't know couldn't hurt her?

What was it she didn't know?

And how could it hurt her?

chapter

8

"And on the left you see the scenic Division Street Mall, with bargain hunters and other exotic life forms. Up ahead and to the right is historic Arnold's Gas Station, open seven days a week. . . ." Max was speaking in a high-pitched, nasal voice, and Jill couldn't help laughing. He sounded exactly like a bored tour guide.

"Just behind us," piped up Nick, also aping a tour guide, "is Mrs. McCormack, the slowest driver in three counties. And over to the left—" He raised his hand to point, and the car suddenly swerved into the next lane.

"Nick, will you keep your eyes on the road!" Jill tried to sound upset, but she was laughing too hard. Andrea, sitting beside her on the seat, was laughing too, and even Diane, sitting on Jill's other side, was giggling.

"Okay, girls, what's next?" Max swiveled his head around from the middle of the front seat. Gabe, sitting next to him, had his head against the door. He seemed to be asleep.

"Ask Gabe," said Andrea. "We've all lived in Shadyside forever. Gabe?"

Gabe stretched and yawned elaborately. "Well, let's see. I've seen the main drag, the river drive, the mall, and a gas station. I don't know if I can take much more."

"Oh, cut it out, Gabe," said Diane, sounding exasperated. "It was *your* idea to cruise by those places, in case you've forgotten."

"Well, yeah, okay," Gabe admitted. "I mean, I've got to be able to find my way around town. But what about that weird place you guys told me about? Fear Street? We never went on it to get to Diane's cabin, remember? We went a roundabout way."

"Fear Street, coming up," said Nick, swinging the wheel around.

As Nick gunned the car down Old Mill Road toward Fear Street, Jill felt a shiver of excitement move down her back.

"You sure you're ready for this, Gabe?" cracked Max. "We're talking serious stuff here. Ghosts, evil spirits, vampires—"

"Bring 'em on!" said Gabe. Then he stuck his head out the window of the car and repeated, at the top of his voice, "Bring 'em on! *I'm ready!*"

Andrea was laughing again, her eyes glued to Gabe. Jill thought it was funny too, but somehow she wasn't so sure he had the right attitude about Fear Street.

After a few minutes the streetlights became more infrequent, and Nick turned onto Fear Street, slowing the wagon to a crawl. "This is it," Max said, resuming his tour-guide voice. "Fear Street. End of the Line."

"This is *it?"* said Gabe in obvious disbelief. "This is your famous haunted street?"

"Doesn't look like much, does it?" said Max. "But appearances can be deceiving. See that house across the street? The one with the green shutters?"

"Yeah?"

"Well, two years ago the police found six human skeletons buried in the backyard."

"Over there are the ruins of Simon Fear's old mansion," said Andrea. "You can just make it out in the dark."

"I'm terrified," said Gabe, sounding anything but.

"Past the cemetery and through the woods back there," said Diane. "See how dark it is? A house burned down during a Halloween party last year and nearly killed everyone in it."

"And some friends of mine were nearly murdered by a nut with a chain saw at that house on the corner," said Jill, getting into the spirit of things.

"I know a girl whose parents disappeared from here," added Nick.

Everyone was talking at once now, remembering stories about Fear Street and the terrible things that had happened on it.

Finally Gabe put his hands over his ears and started laughing. "Whoa!" he said. "You're scaring me to death!"

"But all this stuff is *real,"* said Andrea. "It all really did happen."

"Maybe so," said Gabe. "But to me it just looks like a bunch of old houses. I want to see something really scary."

"Well, we could try the cemetery," said Max doubtfully.

"Awesome!" said Andrea. "I've never been there at night!"

"I've never been there at all," said Diane in a small voice. "Are you sure it's safe, Max?"

"There are six of us, right?" said Max.

"That's not going to stop the *undead*," said Nick, doing his awful Dracula impersonation.

"The what?" said Gabe.

"The undead," said Jill. "That's one of the stories about Fear Street—the undead sometimes come out of their graves in the cemetery and roam through the woods."

"This I've gotta see!" said Gabe. He turned again to the backseat. "You guys don't really believe this stuff, do you?"

"Well, I'm not sure about the undead," Jill admitted, "but there is something very creepy about Fear Street."

"And all those things we told you really happened," added Andrea.

"Well, let's check out the cemetery!" said Gabe.

"Next stop!" said Nick, cutting the engine at the end of the street. Beyond the turnaround loomed the wall of the graveyard.

"Got a flashlight?" asked Diane nervously.

"I don't think so," said Nick. "But I don't think we need one. Look how bright the moon is."

"That's when the undead are supposed to come out," said Andrea, sounding excited. "When there's a full moon."

The six teens got out of the car and started toward the crumbling walls of the cemetery. Jill stood and gazed at it a moment, taking in the fresh night air. From somewhere she caught a whiff of springtime blossoms, and for a moment the cemetery seemed like any other beautiful place in Shadyside.

So why was she suddenly nervous? Why did she have the feeling something bad was about to happen?

The others followed Gabe up to the gate. He knocked on it, then yelled, "Yoo-hoo! Living Dead! Come out, come out, wherever you are!"

"Gabe—get real," said Andrea. No one else said anything.

Gabe unlatched the gate. It swung open with a groan like a cry of pain. The others followed Gabe one at a time. The ground was a tangle of weeds and overgrown grass, and the ancient, crumbling tombstones were covered with moss and scraggly vines.

"They don't spend much on the upkeep for this place, do they?" Gabe observed.

"No one's been buried here in years," Jill told him. "Check out the gravestones. Some of them are really old."

Gabe bent down and brushed moss off the carving on a tall, narrow stone. It was relatively easy to read the engraving in the bright moonlight. "'Dollan—1847,'" he read. "Pretty ancient."

"Some of them are wild," Andrea said. "Hey, look at this one!"

Jill peered over Andrea's shoulder to read, "Edwin Dunphy, Born 1852. Hanged as a Thief 1870."

"Gosh," Andrea said. "He wasn't much older than we are."

"I wonder what he stole," said Nick. "It must have been something really valuable for him to get hanged."

"Justice was much rougher in those days," said Max.

"Right," Andrea cracked. "They probably would have executed *you* for setting the boys' room on fire."

"If they caught me," said Max calmly. Since nearly a week had passed and nothing had happened, Max had stopped worrying about the fire.

"That reminds me," said Gabe, straightening up and dusting off his hands. "You haven't set a fire yet, Nick."

"What?" Nick gaped at him. "What are you talking about?"

"Hey, that's right," said Max. "It's your turn, buddy."

"Give me a break," said Nick. "Setting fires is stupid and dangerous."

"And fun," said Max. "You forgot fun."

Jill was pretty sure the boys were just fooling around, but she remembered how fast things had happened in the cafeteria. "Come on, guys," she said. "It's getting cold. Let's go."

None of the boys paid any attention to her. Diane, standing next to Jill, was quiet, but her eyes were wide with worry.

"Max set a fire," Gabe went on. "He proved he's got guts."

"Good for him," said Nick. "I don't have to prove anything."

"Then what's the problem?" said Max. "It's just a goof."

"Or maybe Nick is afraid," said Gabe deliberately.

For a moment no one said anything. Gabe's gone too far, Jill thought. But Nick just took a deep breath and held it, then turned. "Come on," he said. "Let's go."

"Wait!" said Gabe. Nick turned back warily.

"Maybe you're right, Nick," Gabe said with exaggerated kindness. "Maybe it's not your turn yet. It's my turn. . . ." He scanned the graveyard.

"Gabe—" said Jill. "Please don't. Let's just all get back in the car."

"Don't worry, Jill," said Gabe, turning to her with a smile. "A little fire won't hurt anything. It's completely deserted out here. It won't even get classes canceled." He began to laugh a weird, excited laugh.

"What about that shack over there?" said Max, pointing to a run-down wooden shack.

"It looks like an old caretaker's shack," said Andrea, also sounding excited.

"From the looks of it, no one has used it in years," said Gabe. "I'd probably be doing the town a favor by getting rid of it." He pulled open the door and peered inside. "Perfect," he said. "It's full of old sticks and rags. Ought to burn great." He reached down and pushed the debris into a pile in the center of the tiny room. Then he reached into his pocket and pulled out a lighter.

"Hey, man," said Nick nervously. "You're not really going to do it, are you?"

"You don't think so?" said Gabe. He clicked on the lighter. "Just watch me."

chapter

9

*F*or a moment Gabe just stood there, the flame from the lighter illuminating his face. He was deathly calm and was smiling his familiar mocking smile.

Jill sneaked a glance at the others. Both Andrea and Max were watching with their mouths half open, their eyes sparkling excitedly. Diane's eyes too were shining, but Jill couldn't tell if it was from excitement or fear. Only Nick was scowling. He shook his head and turned away from Gabe.

As for Jill, she wasn't sure what she felt. A part of her was sympathetic to Nick and agreed that fires were dangerous and stupid. But another part was excited and waited eagerly to see if Gabe would really do it.

Gabe slowly stepped forward, then bent down and lit the debris inside the shack. Instantly it blazed up and he jumped back.

"Whoa!" he said. "That stuff was dry!"

"We'd better get out of here!" said Max. "This shack's going to really burn."

"Right," said Gabe. "Come on!"

Laughing like a wild man, he led the others back through the cemetery and down to where the car was parked.

"That was awesome!" said Max, turning back to watch the shack, which was now blazing brightly.

"I didn't think you'd really do it," said Andrea, putting her hand on Gabe's arm. "I should have known that you mean exactly what you say."

"You bet I do," said Gabe. "Now there's only one detail that needs to be tied up."

"What's that?" said Andrea.

"Nick," said Gabe. "Hey, buddy, now it's definitely your turn!"

They stood for a moment watching the glow of the fire from behind the cemetery wall. Jill found herself thinking it wasn't that big a deal. As Gabe pointed out, they hadn't hurt anyone. And the shack itself was so run-down it was useless.

Even Diane seemed relatively relaxed about what had happened.

Only Nick was still uptight. He was standing off by himself, facing away from the cemetery, his hands in his pockets. Jill was about to walk over to him when a siren began to wail.

"Uh-oh," said Andrea. "Someone called the fire department."

"Too bad," said Gabe. "Hey, Nick, you're going to have to drive past the fire trucks now. Or are you too chicken for that too?"

Nick acted as if he hadn't heard Gabe, but he did head for the car.

The sirens were louder now. They all scrambled

quickly into the car. Jill found herself in the front between Max and Nick, while Gabe was in the back between Andrea and Diane.

"Drive carefully, Nick," Gabe said sarcastically as they started back down Fear Street. "You wouldn't want to do something illegal and get a ticket."

The others all laughed, except for Nick. Jill thought Gabe was being too hard on him. He didn't realize how sensitive Nick was. If I could just talk to Gabe alone, she thought. Maybe Saturday night when we go out.

She still hadn't told anyone she was going out with Gabe, and she wondered if he would say anything.

"Here they come!" cried Max jubilantly.

Nick pulled over while the fire trucks passed, their blaring sirens shattering the quiet of Fear Street.

"I still haven't seen any of the undead," complained Gabe.

"They were probably afraid of *you*," said Max.

"Could be," said Gabe.

"You never know," said Diane. "Maybe they put a curse on you."

"Come to think of it, I scraped my hand when I was piling stuff up inside the shack," Gabe said. "Think that's the curse?"

"Let me kiss it and take the curse off," said Andrea. While the others whistled and hooted, she took Gabe's hand in hers and put it to her mouth.

What would she say if she knew Gabe asked me out? Jill wondered.

"Hey, Andrea," teased Max, "you never did that for any of us."

Everyone laughed. Jill had never seen Andrea act so

flirtatious. It was as if the fires brought out a side of her no one knew existed.

"Say, Gabe," Andrea said huskily, "when are you going to come watch my gymnastics routine?"

"I haven't had much time this week," said Gabe.

"How about Saturday night?" Andrea said.

"I'm busy that night," Gabe said smoothly. "How about next Thursday?"

"You're on," said Andrea.

Nick turned south on Old Mill Road, heading around the woods. He switched on a heavy-metal tape and cranked it up loud. For a few minutes no one spoke as the music reverberated inside the old car. Jill closed her eyes, listening to the beat, feeling the wind from the outside rush by her face.

As Nick approached the on-ramp for the interstate he slowed, then turned the car around. "What now?" he said, switching off the tape.

"Let's take a vote," said Jill. "It's not too late to see a movie, or we could go to Pete's for pizza, or—" There was no immediate answer, and Max nudged her, then pointed to the rearview mirror.

Jill glanced up and felt her heart turn over. Reflected in the mirror were Gabe and Andrea locked in a steamy kiss.

chapter
10

The music died as the credits rolled, and Andrea clicked the TV off, then set the VCR to rewind. "Now, that," she said, "was a terrific movie. That guy—the blond-haired biker? Was he cute or what?"

"He was pretty cute," Jill agreed. "But there was something just a little too wild about him for me."

"That's what I liked," said Andrea. She turned to Diane, who was curled up in a beanbag chair. "Di? What'd you think of the movie?"

Diane shrugged. "It was all right." She had hardly spoken a word all evening.

Jill looked around Andrea's room. It was small, but had everything anyone could want, all built in—TV, VCR, CD player. Everything was in modular cabinets, which were closed and neat except when Andrea was using the equipment.

The machine finished rewinding and clicked off. Andrea pointed at the stack of remaining tapes. "What do you want to see next?"

"What've we got?" said Jill.

"A dumb comedy and a dumb action-adventure movie," said Andrea. "I never heard of either one. My dad rented them."

"I vote for the dumb comedy," said Jill. "Diane?"

"I don't care," said Diane.

"Hey, Miss Enthusiasm," said Andrea. "If I'd known you were going to be so much fun tonight, I'd have invited a bowl of oatmeal to sleep over instead."

"Sorry," said Diane. She settled deeper in the beanbag.

For a moment there was an awkward silence. Jill couldn't imagine what was wrong with Diane.

"Okay, I've got an idea," said Andrea. "Let's forget the videos for a while and listen to music. I've got a couple of new CDs."

"Sounds good," said Jill.

Andrea hopped up and popped a CD into the player.

"It was nice of your dad to let us sleep over," Jill said.

"He just made me promise there'd be no—get this—*loud giggling*," Andrea said. At that all three girls—even Diane—started to giggle.

Andrea's mother had been out of town on business for a week, and Jill suspected Andrea had her father twisted around her little finger.

"I almost forgot. I've got to show you what Dad got me for an early birthday present," said Andrea. "You're not going to believe this." She went to the modular desk unit in the corner and opened the door, revealing a new laptop computer and printer.

"Wow!" said Jill. "Look how little it is!"

"It's got lots of power," said Andrea. "It can do

calculations and play games, and it's got a word processor. Dad thinks it'll help me with my grades."

"Turn it on," said Diane. "Let's see you print something out."

Andrea switched on the computer, then put a disk in. After a few seconds the disk booted, and the cursor blinked, ready for input.

"What'll I write?" said Andrea.

"Anything," said Jill.

"A poem," said Diane.

"Are you kidding?" said Andrea. "Well, why not." She thought a moment, then began to tap on the keys. After a few minutes she pressed a function key. Instantly the printer began stuttering and ejected a short message in bright blue ink.

> I hope you won't think I'm a liar,
> But I love it when Gabe plays with fire.

"Blue ink?" said Jill.

"My dad got a blue cartridge by mistake," said Andrea. "He offered to take it back, but I like the way it looks, don't you?"

"It's different," said Jill. "I'm not so sure about the poem, though."

"Hey, what do you expect," said Andrea. "I'm not a writer. But I do think it's true that computers make you more creative."

"You don't really believe that, do you?" asked Diane suddenly.

"Believe what?"

"What you said in the poem. About fire?"

"Well, sure—I don't know," said Andrea. "It was

just something I thought of on the spur of the moment. It's no big deal."

"I think it's a bigger deal than you realize," said Diane. "Did you two see the article in the paper today?"

"You mean the article about all the fires?" said Jill.

"Today?" said Andrea. "I didn't see it."

"It wasn't on the front page or anything," said Jill, "but there was an article about how there's been an increase in arson in Shadyside. It specifically mentioned fires at the school and in the cemetery."

"Wow!" whooped Andrea, her face suddenly flushed with excitement. "We made the paper!"

"Luckily," Jill went on, "they don't seem to suspect anyone in particular."

"That's just too much," Andrea said. "I wonder if the guys know?"

"Gabe knows," said Diane. Her voice sounded strained and upset. "He's the one who told me about it."

"What does he think?" said Andrea.

"He feels the same way about it you do!" said Diane, her voice suddenly angry. "He sees it all as some sort of game! But it's not! Someone could get in real trouble—or get hurt."

Jill and Andrea both stared at Diane. Jill knew how much Diane feared fire, but she never realized until now how serious she was about it.

"It has to stop," Diane went on. "The whole fire thing."

"In other words," said Andrea sarcastically, "just because sweet little Diane doesn't like fire, the rest of us have to stop having fun?"

"Andrea, there are plenty of ways to have fun without setting fires," said Diane.

"Maybe so," said Andrea. "But I don't know who said you can dictate to the rest of us what we do and don't do."

"Fine," said Diane. "But if you guys are going to keep setting fires, then I'm not going to hang out with you anymore."

"Hey, girls, come on!" Jill had been listening to the argument with growing concern. She had to admit she'd been just as excited as everyone else by the fires, but she thought Diane had a point. "Diane's right, Andrea," she said, trying to placate her friend. "This fire game could get someone in a lot of trouble."

"Great," said Andrea. "Now you're on her side too!"

"I'm not on anyone's side. But—we've been good friends for a long time, and I don't want to see anything break that up. Besides, I think the guys are getting too competitive about setting fires."

"You mean Gabe's the only one with any guts."

"Gabe takes it too seriously," said Jill. "They all do. That's the whole point. I think we ought to tell them to stop it."

"They'll listen to you, Jill," said Diane. "I know they will."

"I don't know," said Andrea. She had begun painting her fingernails and seemed bored with the whole discussion.

Jill was trying to think of another argument to use on Andrea when the phone rang.

"Will one of you get that?" asked Andrea. She was holding her hands in front of her face, blowing on the nails as they dried.

Jill picked up Andrea's red Trimline phone. "Hello?"

"Is this Miss Andrea Hubbard?" said a gruff, official-sounding voice.

"She's busy right now," said Jill. "May I take a message?"

"Just tell her," said the gruff voice, "that this is Inspector Lindsay of the Shadyside Fire Department. We want to ask her some questions about a suspected case of arson."

chapter

11

For a moment Jill felt as if her heart had stopped.

They've found us! she thought.

"Jill? What is it?" Diane was staring at her with alarm.

Jill waved at her to be quiet. "Who did you say you are?" she asked, hoping she had heard wrong.

"Inspector Lindsay," repeated the voice, "of the Shadyside Fire Department." His voice cracked slightly, and Jill felt relief flood through her. Relief and anger.

"Max, you dork!" she shouted.

"I don't know any Max," said Max. "This is Inspector—"

"I know it's you!" Jill cut in. "And you're very funny. As funny as a coffin!"

"How's the slumber party, girls?" It was Nick's voice on Max's other phone.

"Everything's just peachy!" said Jill sarcastically.

"And I don't remember anyone inviting you!" She hung up the phone before either boy could say more.

"What did Max want?" asked Andrea, applying a coat of quick dryer.

"He wanted to show how clever he is," said Jill. "He said he was a fire inspector. But the awful part is—for a minute I believed him!"

"What a dweeb," said Andrea.

"Maybe," said Jill. "But it could have been real. Now, are we going to stop this stupid fire game—or not?"

Andrea sighed. "Oh, all right. I guess it wouldn't hurt to cool things awhile—especially now that the police are looking into arson."

"Thank heaven!" said Diane, smiling broadly. "Thanks, both of you." She quickly hugged each of her friends in turn. "This is the best thing for all of us. You'll see!"

She picked up her pink overnight bag and disappeared into the bathroom.

Andrea shook her head. "I guess I didn't realize before how strongly Diane felt about fire."

"I didn't either," said Jill.

"In fact," said Andrea, "it's hard to believe she and Gabe are such good friends."

"Why do you say that?"

"They're just two completely different people," said Andrea. "The fire thing is only part of it. Diane's shy, Gabe's outgoing—he's really much more your type—or mine."

It's now or never, Jill thought. "I've been meaning to talk to you about Gabe," she said. "I'm . . . going out with him tomorrow night."

"Really?" said Andrea. She didn't seem at all upset. "Well, that's very interesting, because he's spending next Thursday afternoon and evening with me to work on the music for my floor routine."

"Well, that's great," said Jill.

"Except," Andrea added, "I'm planning to work on a lot more than my routine." She looked Jill in the eye, then flashed her a mischievous smile. "Have a good time tomorrow night, Jill. Just keep in mind that I'm not backing off. As they used to say in the movies, may the best man—or woman—win."

The moon was just past full, and all around it a million stars were shining. A soft breeze floated the scent of spring flowers, and Jill thought it was the most romantic evening she had ever spent in her life.

Across from her, sitting on a picnic table, Gabe was softly strumming his guitar, his eyes closed as he sang a slow, sad song. With the moonlight shining on his face, he looked very handsome, Jill thought. There wasn't a trace of the wild Gabe, just the sensitive one.

When he picked her up, she wondered how he would behave around her parents. But he had been, as her mother would put it, a perfect gentleman. He had even held the car door open for her, which was strange and sweet at the same time.

What a perfect evening, she thought. The movie had been great, but even better had been Gabe's idea of going to the park so that he could play music just for her. I'll never forget this evening, she thought.

Gabe finished the song, then set the guitar down.

"That was great," said Jill. "Did you write it?"

"I'm still working on it," said Gabe with a smile. "You like it?"

"It's better than most of the stuff they play on the radio," she said.

Gabe crossed to the bench where she was sitting and sat beside her. "I've had a nice time tonight," he said.

"Me too," she said.

"Hanging out with the other kids is fun," he went on, "but I've been wanting to get to know you alone."

Jill couldn't think of what to say. She felt the same way, but somehow it didn't seem right to say so. Very casually, Gabe took her hand.

"So, what is the real Jill Franks like?" he asked, only half-teasing.

"I think," she said, "that I'm just the way I seem to be."

He was silent a moment. "I think that's true. A lot of people wear masks, or put on an act, but you seem to be just you."

"What about you?" Jill said. "Do you have a mask?"

Again Gabe fell silent. "What do you think?" he said at last.

"I'm not sure," said Jill. "But you seem so different now than when we're hanging out with the others."

"Yeah?" he asked. "Which me do you like better?"

"Both of them," said Jill. "I like the way you always want to do something exciting. But I also like it when you just sit and play music and talk."

"Well, maybe I'd better do that more often," he said. Without letting go of her hand, he put his other hand on the back of her neck. Jill felt first as if her heart had stopped, and then felt it pounding furiously. Never had she felt this way about a boy.

"I think I'm starting to be glad my folks moved to Shadyside," Gabe whispered.

"I'm glad too," said Jill.

Very gently Gabe kissed her.

I want to stay here in this park with Gabe forever, she thought. I don't ever want this moment to end.

Gabe kissed her again.

"Tumbler!" called a cracked voice. "Here, Tumbler!"

A bright light suddenly went on, and Jill blinked against it, turning her head. "What're you—oops, excuse me." It was Mr. Morrissey, who owned the deli across the street. He switched off the flashlight. "Sorry to bother you. My dog got out. Don't suppose you've seen him, have you?"

"No," said Gabe. "But we weren't really looking for him."

"I guess not," said Mr. Morrissey. He chuckled. "Well, sorry to disturb you. Tumbler!" he called, walking off. "Here, Tumbler!"

"On the other hand," Gabe said, laughing, "Shadyside is a very weird place."

Jill laughed too. The magic moment had been broken, but it didn't seem to matter.

"Hey," said Gabe, checking his watch. "It's later than I thought. I'd better get you home. Don't want to get your folks mad at me on our first date."

First date, Jill thought. That means he wants to go out with me again.

Gabe packed his guitar into its case, then picked it up, and taking Jill's hand began to walk with her out of the park.

"I've had a great time, Gabe," Jill said. "There's just one thing I want to talk to you about." She hesitated to bring up the fire game, but she and the other girls had agreed. Besides, she was a little worried about Nick.

"Sure," said Gabe. "What is it?" They were parked near Pete's Pizza, which was two blocks away.

"It's about the fire—the fire game," Jill said.

"The fire game? Is that what you call it?" asked Gabe. "Well, what about it?"

"Andrea and Diane and I had a serious talk about it, and—and, we want it to stop."

"Are you serious?" Gabe stopped walking to turn to her, the old mocking smile on his face. "Why?"

"Because it's dangerous and illegal, and we're afraid someone's going to get in trouble. Besides, I think the other boys are taking it too seriously. Especially Nick."

Gabe shook his head. "No way, Jill," he said, smiling at her. *You're* the one who's taking it seriously. It's just a goof. And it's not like we're running around setting fire to everything we see."

"Well, but—" Now Jill was confused.

"But nothing," said Gabe. "If you're so worried about the other guys, ask them how they feel about it. They'll tell you the same thing I just did. Come on, now. Chill out."

"Oh, Gabe," she said. "Maybe you're right."

"Sure I am," he said. They started walking again. The way he put it, it didn't seem that serious. She and Diane were both overreacting.

They turned the corner onto Main Street. There was a big crowd in front of Pete's Pizza. "I've never seen a line like that," said Jill. "They must be having a sale on pepperoni or something."

"I wish we had time to check it out," said Gabe.

But as they got closer, Jill saw that the crowd wasn't waiting to get into Pete's at all. "Gabe, it's a fire! Someone's car is on fire!"

Gabe saw it too. "Hey—it's my car! Hold this!" He handed her the guitar and began sprinting down the block.

"Gabe!" she shouted. Holding the guitar awkwardly at her side, she ran after him. The car was blazing furiously, the interior a mass of red and yellow flames. The crowd had started to move back from the intense heat.

"Get back!" someone shouted. "It's going to blow."

But Gabe was running directly toward the fire. "I've got to do something!" he cried.

"Gabe, no!" Jill dropped the guitar and ran after him as fast as she could. She threw her arms around him from the back. He struggled with her like a crazy person and broke away from her.

"No!" she shouted. "Stop! Gabe! Come back!"

An instant later the fire reached the gas tank. With a deafening roar the car exploded.

chapter

12

Jill stood in the crowd, holding Gabe's guitar, behind a wooden barrier the fire fighters had set up. The ruined hulk of the car continued to smolder, and the air was filled with the stench of burned rubber and gasoline.

In front of the barricade, Gabe, his clothes and face still covered with dust and soot from being blown to the sidewalk when the car exploded, was talking to the fire chief and two police officers. She couldn't hear what they were saying, but Gabe was gesturing angrily, pacing and shaking his head. She had never seen him so upset.

Why did this have to happen? she asked herself. Everything had been so perfect.

Finally the officials finished with Gabe and he came back to Jill. "I don't believe it!" he said. "They wanted to know if *I* set the car on fire!"

"They probably have to ask questions like that," said Jill.

"Why would I do it?" he went on. "And it's not even my car! It's my father's!"

"I'm so sorry," Jill said. "I'm sure he'll understand it wasn't your fault."

"He's only had the car a few months," Gabe went on. "I can't believe it!" He began to pace up and down the sidewalk. "Do you know what the fire chief said? He said they won't know for sure till the car cools down, but it looks like arson."

"Arson!" Jill tried to sound shocked, but she wasn't really. "Who would do such a thing? And why?"

"Why is easy," said Gabe. "Jealousy. As for who—well, I have some ideas about that."

An hour later Jill sat staring at her telephone, feeling cold and sick inside.

"The fire game has to stop," she said out loud.

Ever since Gabe had told her that the fire chief suspected arson, Jill had known who set the fire.

It was Nick.

It had to be.

It was his "turn," after all. Gabe hadn't let him forget it for a minute.

Even worse, Gabe suspected Nick too. Diane must have told him how Nick felt about Jill. But could he really have done such a terrible thing out of jealousy?

Maybe Gabe had really pushed Nick too far the other night.

In any case, Jill meant to find out.

She picked up the phone and punched in Nick's number.

"Hello?" Nick's voice sounded groggy.

"Nick, it's Jill," she said.

"Oh, yeah? How you doing? What time is it?"

"It's a little past midnight," she said. Then she took a deep breath and plunged right in. "Nick, how can you possibly sleep after what you did?"

"Huh?"

"I know what you did tonight," she went on. "Don't bother to deny it."

"Why should I deny it?" said Nick, sounding slightly more awake. "I was home alone all night. I watched *The Fly*—the old one *and* the new one."

"You did more than that."

"What are you talking about?" Nick sounded genuinely puzzled.

"Nick, I know that you set the fire. It had to be you."

"What fire?"

"Are you denying that you set Gabe's car on fire?"

"Someone set Gabe's car on fire?" said Nick. Then suddenly his voice turned angry. "Of course I deny it! How can you accuse me?"

"Well," said Jill, "it was your turn next. Everyone knows that."

"Well, you're not supposed to be everyone! You're supposed to be my friend."

"Nick, it's okay," Jill pleaded. "You can tell me. I just called because I think the fires have to stop."

"I didn't set the fire," said Nick, "and if you don't believe me, that's your problem!"

Jill was about to protest again, but before she could, Nick hung up on her.

Suddenly Jill was worried about more than just the fire game. She was worried about Nick too. This whole thing had gone much too far.

She glanced nervously at her bedside clock, then decided to call Andrea. She was never going to be able to sleep anyway, and Andrea usually stayed up late watching TV.

"Hello?" With relief, Jill heard Andrea's wide-awake voice.

"Hi, it's Jill," she said.

"What are you doing home so soon?" said Andrea. "I thought you had a date with Gabe tonight."

"Well, I did," said Jill. "And that's what I want to talk to you about."

"I hope you're not going to ask me to break my date with him," said Andrea. "Because I won't."

"No, no," said Jill. "Listen to me. Something terrible happened. There was another fire."

"Really?" Andrea sounded interested. "What did he set on fire this time?"

"It wasn't Gabe who set the fire," Jill said. "It was Nick. At least, I think it was. He set Gabe's car on fire. It exploded."

"Really?" Andrea sounded even more interested. "That must have been awesome. I wish I'd been there."

"It wasn't awesome. It was horrible," said Jill. "Gabe was so upset I couldn't even talk to him, and Nick denies that he did it, and I just don't know what to do."

"Hey, calm down. You sound really upset."

"I am. Andrea, we've got to make the guys stop setting fires."

"What do you want to do? Follow them around with a fire extinguisher?"

"Andrea—"

"Though come to think of it," Andrea went on, "I wouldn't mind following Gabe around. . . ."

"Will you be serious?"

72

"I am serious," Andrea said. "But I don't really think it's as big a deal as you think it is. I mean, sure, it's terrible that Gabe's car burned up, but maybe it'll all stop now. After all, they've each set one fire."

"True," said Jill.

"Anyway, there's nothing we can do about it to-night. What I'd really like to talk about is your—excuse the expression—hot date. Except for the fire, how was it?"

"It was nice," Jill said, suddenly feeling very sad. "It was nicer than I expected it to be."

"But the fire ruined things? Is that what you're saying?"

"Sort of," Jill admitted.

"Well, too bad," Andrea said. "Maybe I'll be luckier when I see Gabe on Thursday."

"Yeah, maybe," Jill said. "Well, I'll talk to you tomorrow."

After she hung up, Jill felt worse than ever. She got ready for bed, then pulled the covers up and closed her eyes. She tried to remember how wonderful she had felt with Gabe in the park, but the memory was already fading. When she tried to picture him playing the guitar and singing to her, all she could visualize was his angry expression after the car burned.

What would happen when he went out with Andrea? she wondered. Would he sing the same songs to her, hold her hand, kiss Andrea the way he had kissed her?

And what about the fire game? Would it really be over now, as Andrea predicted?

Much later, Jill was awakened by a familiar—and now terrifying—smell: smoke. Her heart thudding in her chest, she sat straight up in bed. No, she thought. Not here. It can't be.

The smell grew stronger, and she realized she had to warn her parents. She opened her mouth to scream, but no sound would come out. It was as if the smoke were choking her, choking back her voice.

Feeling faint and weak, she struggled out of bed and down the hall, calling to her parents, but the sound that came out was only a feeble squeak.

More frightened than ever, she pulled open their bedroom door and saw their bed empty.

No!

She was alone.

Alone with the fire.

She turned and ran down the hall. The reflection of red and orange flames came from somewhere downstairs. She stumbled down the stairs, fighting for breath with every step, feeling as if her body weighed a thousand pounds.

The glow of the fire was coming from the kitchen. Terrified, yet drawn to it, she followed the glow and saw that flames were coming out of the stove.

Frantic, she ran for the bucket in the closet, then filled it with water and poured it over the stove. Again and again she filled the bucket and doused the fire. Finally it sputtered and sizzled out. The stove in front of her was blackened with soot.

Terrified of what she would find, she opened the oven, where the fire seemed to have started.

"Oh, no! No! Please—no!" There, black and charred, lay the body of Mittsy.

chapter
13

With her own scream ringing in her ears, Jill sat bolt upright in bed.

It had been a nightmare. A dreadfully vivid nightmare.

Mittsy was alive and well, curled up next to her on the covers.

She clutched the soft little cat and hugged her close.

I'll never get back to sleep, she thought. She got up and went downstairs to the kitchen. There was no trace of fire. Not the slightest smell of smoke.

She opened the refrigerator and poured a glass of milk.

It was only a dream, she thought again. A nightmare. But part of the nightmare was real. The part that had to do with the fire game.

It had to stop. It just had to.

I hate algebra, Jill thought, staring at a page full of mysterious symbols. It was going to take her the entire study period just to get started on these stupid problems. "I hate it," she whispered aloud.

Behind her, someone whispered in her ear, "What do you hate?" It was Nick. It was the first thing he'd said to her since he hung up on her the other night.

"Algebra," Jill said, surprised and relieved. "I hate algebra."

"It's not so bad," whispered Nick, slipping into the empty seat beside her. "You just have to look at it the right way. I bet you were never good at fractions, were you?"

"No," said Jill. "But so what? I'm just missing the part of the brain that does math."

"Probably," agreed Nick. He looked up, then was silent a moment as Mr. Borden, the study-hall monitor, walked by. When the teacher had gone, he resumed whispering. "Hey, bet I can show you some things about fractions that will make algebra a snap."

"Really?" Jill couldn't help smiling. "I'll believe it when I see it. But if it works, it would be great."

"It'll work," said Nick. "Why don't you come over to my house tonight and we can get started?"

Jill thought a moment. "Sure. Why not? Thanks, Nick."

Driving over to Nick's house, Jill felt optimistic once again. Not only was she going to get help with her algebra, she might also be able to talk to Nick about the fire game. To get him to promise never to set another fire.

She'd decided that was the best way to do it—to get the guys one by one to agree to stop.

Nick really liked her, and even if he *had* set Gabe's car on fire, she was sure he would listen to her.

She turned the corner onto Front Street and was about to pull up in front of Nick's house when she saw a familiar car backing out of the driveway.

It was Nick's father's station wagon, and Nick and Max were in the front seat.

"Hey!" she called, rolling down the window. "Hey, guys!"

Either they didn't hear her or they were deliberately ignoring her, because the car continued roaring down the street.

What's going on? she wondered. Had Nick forgotten the study date, or was he playing some kind of mean trick on her?

She decided to find out.

Staying behind the brown station wagon but not getting too close to it, she started to follow the boys. At first she was afraid that they would see her, but they were busy talking to each other, not paying any attention to who might be behind them.

For a moment, going through the center of town, she lost the car, but then picked it up again as it turned north on Old Mill Road.

Where are they going? she wondered.

She continued to follow the car until Nick signaled for a right turn onto Fear Street.

It was a dark, cloudy night, and the area seemed to be more deserted than ever. The street lamp at the corner of Old Mill Road and Fear Street had burned out, and huge shadows grew on every side of her.

I don't really need to follow them anymore, Jill thought. I know they've gone to Fear Street.

But she still didn't know why, and she had an idea it might be important.

She pulled the car over and checked to make sure all the doors were locked, then turned onto Fear Street.

There was no sign of the wagon or the boys. It was as if they had disappeared into a black hole. Worried, she squinted to see as far down the street as she could.

They must have pulled into a driveway somewhere, she thought. The only thing she could do was cruise the street, checking out each driveway as she passed.

Driving as slowly as she could, Jill headed down the deserted street in the direction of the cemetery. Somehow, all alone in the dark, it seemed much scarier than it had the other night with her friends. She remembered some of the stories they'd been telling about the terrible things that had happened in the different houses, and she felt a shiver pass through her.

She studied each house she came to, but there was no sign of the boys. They had to be here. Fear Street was a dead-end street. There was no way out.

Dead end.

No way out.

Stop it, Jill told herself. She took a deep breath and kept driving. Suddenly her car started to shudder and then the engine died.

"No!" Jill cried aloud in annoyance.

Again and again she turned the key, stepping on the gas. But nothing happened.

Somewhere off to the right a large figure came bounding across a yard and disappeared toward the woods.

It was a dog, Jill told herself. Just a dog.

She felt a trickle of perspiration run down her forehead.

This is ridiculous, she told herself. There's nothing

to be scared of. I'm in a locked car. I'm only a block from Old Mill Road. If the car doesn't start soon, I can walk back and phone for help.

Please start, she thought, turning the key again.

The engine cranked and cranked, but wouldn't catch.

I've probably flooded it, she thought. I'll just have to wait for a few minutes before I try again.

A bat fluttered against a dim streetlight across the street, and Jill gasped. Now, suddenly, the deep shadows seemed to have a life of their own. She thought she could see things moving at the corner of her vision. But whenever she turned to stare directly at them, there was nothing there.

Except in her rearview mirror.

Glancing up, Jill saw a dark figure moving toward her car.

Her heart pounding, she turned around. She couldn't see any details in the gloom, but there was definitely someone there, walking up the street toward her car.

Maybe it's someone who lives here, she thought. Someone out for an evening stroll.

Maybe.

But in that case, why was he coming directly toward her car?

Wildly, she turned the key and tried to get the engine to catch. But she had no more luck than she had before.

A second later something hit hard against her window and she was blinded by a glaring light.

chapter

14

*F*ighting down choking panic, Jill tried to think what to do. There was no way the car would start, but maybe she could find something—a weapon of some sort.

Frantically she looked around the front seat and floor, then opened the glove compartment. There was nothing but the driver's manual and a half-eaten chocolate bar.

If only the light weren't so bright.

Whatever had hit her window hit it again, then continued in a rhythmic tattoo.

Suddenly Jill realized that it was someone knocking on her window and asking her to open it. No way I'll do that, she thought. But she did roll it down a crack, just enough to talk through.

"Are you all right, miss?" asked the figure. He turned his flashlight to his face, and Jill saw that it was a young police officer.

Relief flooded through her. "I'm fine," she said in a

small voice, "but my car stalled and I can't get it started."

"Let me take a look," said the officer. "Can you unlatch the hood?"

Jill reached for the hood latch and popped it. The police officer disappeared behind the hood. A few minutes later he came back. "Everything seems to be fine," he said. "Do you mind unlocking the door?"

"Well," said Jill. He certainly looked like a policeman, and he acted like a policeman. But she'd heard stories of people impersonating cops and then robbing their victims—or worse.

"You're right to be cautious," the young cop said. "Let me show you my ID." He reached into his pocket and took out a picture ID, then slipped it in to her through the window. Jill scrutinized it, comparing it with his face.

He was definitely a cop. She had never felt so relieved in her whole life. She unlocked the door, then slid over as the cop sat down next to her. He turned the key, and to Jill's surprise the car started right up.

"It wouldn't start before. Honest," she said, feeling like an idiot.

"Probably you flooded it," he said. "While I was checking the engine it had enough time to dry out."

"Well, thank you very much," said Jill.

"My pleasure," said the officer. "I hope you get where you're going soon. This isn't the best neighborhood to be driving around in alone."

"I know," Jill agreed. "Thank you, Officer."

In her fright Jill had almost forgotten why she was there. She waited for the officer to get back into his patrol car and drive away, then resumed her search for Nick and Max.

She had almost reached the cemetery, with no sign of them, when suddenly she spotted their station wagon parked in the yard of a run-down, deserted-looking house just at the edge of the woods.

What in the world could the guys be doing there?

She cut the engine and sat watching the house for a few minutes. They had to come out sooner or later.

But then what? Would she confront them, or follow them again? She reminded herself that she'd followed them to find out what they were up to. She'd never have a better chance than now.

She took a deep breath, then unlocked the door and climbed out. The air was cool, and she realized with a start that she wasn't wearing a jacket. Somewhere off in the woods an animal howled.

Shivering, she began to make her way toward the deserted house.

In the dark it was hard to keep her footing, and she had to move slowly to avoid being tripped by a rock or overgrown vine. There was no sign of life in the house, and as she got closer she could see that most of the windows were broken, jagged shards of glass hanging from their frames like icicles.

What are the boys doing here? she wondered again.

She heard a loud thumping from inside the house and stopped in fright. She was about to start moving toward it again when there was a sudden brilliant flash and the house erupted into flames.

Squinting against the sudden brightness, she saw Nick and Max running at top speed toward the car parked out front.

chapter

15

As Jill watched, horrified, the fire spread until the house seemed to be the center of one large flame. She could hear the crackling and popping of burning wood, and she felt the heat, even out there by the street.

Through the smoke she saw the brown station wagon pull out of the yard, and then roar off down the street. There was too much smoke for her to see her friends' faces, but she imagined they both were laughing.

Jill pulled into the garage but didn't make a move to get out of the car. In her mind's eye she could still see Max and Nick running away from the fire on Fear Street—the fire they had set.

She was pretty sure that they hadn't seen her there. Maybe they didn't care if she *had* seen them. Obviously, they had gotten out of control as far as the fire game was concerned.

After Nick and Max had driven off, Jill had gone

directly to the fire box on Old Mill Road and pulled the alarm. Then she drove around for a while until she finally decided she had to go home to figure out what to do next.

Part of the reason she was so upset, she realized, was that the fire game had changed her relationship with all her friends. There wasn't even anyone she could discuss it with. Max and Andrea both acted as if there were nothing wrong with setting fires. And because of Gabe, she didn't feel comfortable confiding in Andrea anyway.

Diane was completely irrational on the subject of fire. And Nick—Nick was the biggest problem of all. He had been the one who had seemed completely against the fires from the start. Now he had just set *two* fires.

She locked the car and went in. Her parents were out, so she poured herself a glass of tomato juice, then took Mittsy up to her room. She hugged her pet for a while, then decided to study to take her mind off the fire game—and her feelings of guilt about it.

But when she sat down at her desk, the first thing she saw was her algebra book, which she'd brought in from the car. It reminded her of Nick, and how he'd gone to set a fire instead of studying with her that night.

"I give up!" she cried irritably, shutting the book.

She decided to do yoga exercises to calm down. She switched on the little portable TV she kept on her dresser, then sat on the rug and stretched to the sounds of canned laughter as an old episode of "Three's Company" came to an end.

She was doing a shoulder stand when the news came on. "The governor vetoes a capital punishment bill," said the anchorperson. "A homeless man dies in a suspicious fire. And more warm weather ahead. These stories and more coming up on 'Metro News Tonight.'"

Jill continued to stretch, half-listening to the news. She was just starting a half-forward twist when the anchor said, "Police suspect arson in a fatal fire tonight in Shadyside. For more on the story, we go to Tip Teppler."

Jill stopped stretching and sat up straight, her heart thudding.

The TV showed a handsome man with styled blond hair holding a microphone. In the background could be seen a confusion of fire trucks and the blackened silhouette of a burned house. "Thank you, Heidi," said the reporter. "I'm reporting from Fear Street in Shadyside, where fire fighters struggled for nearly two hours to contain a fire in an abandoned house. Fire fighters arriving on the scene found a homeless man unconscious on the front porch. Efforts to revive him at the scene failed, and he was pronounced dead on arrival at Mercy Hospital, the apparent victim of a heart attack. With me is Lieutenant Ed Heasly, chief fire warden for the Shadyside Fire Department. Lieutenant, is it true that this fire was deliberately set?"

The camera switched to another man, this one weary looking, with rumpled, thinning brown hair. "It looks that way, Tip," said Lieutenant Heasly. "We won't know until we complete our investigation, but the fire appears to have been deliberately set."

"Isn't it true," Tip Teppler went on, "that there has been an increase in arson in Shadyside in the last few weeks?"

"That's true also," said Heasly. "We're currently pursuing several leads, but we can't say more right now. I can tell you this. Since this fire involves a death, we aren't going to rest until we find the arsonists."

"Thank you, Lieutenant Heasly," the reporter said. "This is Tip Teppler reporting live from Shadyside. Now back to you in the studio, Heidi."

Feeling dizzy, Jill switched off the set.

The reporter had been standing in front of the house she herself had visited earlier that evening. The house that Nick and Max had set on fire.

The house that wasn't deserted at all, but had had a homeless man living in it.

A homeless man who was now dead.

The reporter said that the man had died of a heart attack, but firemen had found him unconscious. That meant that the fire had caused his death, directly or indirectly.

And it meant that Max and Nick were murderers.

And she was a witness.

chapter

___

16

For a long time Jill stared at the blank television screen. Then she picked up the phone and, her heart thudding, punched in Nick's number.

"Hello?" He sounded sleepy but completely normal. Maybe he hadn't heard about the homeless man yet.

"Hi, this is Jill," she said. "I—I was just calling to find out why you weren't home for our study date."

"Oh!" said Nick, sounding surprised. Then he quickly went on. "I'm sorry, but Max got last-minute tickets to the basketball game in Waynesbridge. I tried to call you, but your line was busy."

"That's really lame, Nick," she said.

"Hey, I'm sorry," he said. "I'll make it up to you. I'll come over tomorrow and—"

"I mean your lie is lame!" she interrupted. "You didn't go to any basketball game tonight, did you?"

"Sure I did," Nick said. "Just ask Max."

"It's bad enough hearing it from you. I don't want

87

to hear the same lies from Max. You didn't go to the basketball game. You went to Fear Street."

Nick didn't answer for a moment. When he did he sounded cautious. "What makes you think so?"

"I saw you there," she said.

"You saw me there?"

"At the house. The one that you and Max set on fire."

"I don't know what you're talking about," Nick said.

Jill thought he sounded very nervous. "Did you see the news on TV tonight?" she asked.

"No. But what does that have to do with—"

"It so happens that there was a homeless man living in that house," Jill said. "And the fire caused his death!"

"What!" Nick sounded shocked. "This is a joke, right?"

"It's no joke," Jill said sadly. "I saw it on the news. They had a picture of the house. It was the same one. The one where I saw you and Max."

"Oh, no," Nick said. "I can't believe it. Someone died?"

"The fire caused him to have a heart attack," Jill said. "And the fire chief said they're looking for the people who did it. You and Max."

"We didn't set the fire!" Nick blurted out.

"Then you admit you were there?"

"We were there," said Nick, "but we didn't set any fire."

"What were you doing there?" asked Jill. Even though she had known Nick was lying before, for some reason she believed him when he said he hadn't set the fire.

"This is going to sound crazy," said Nick. "And if the police ever find us, they'll never believe us!"

"Calm down," Jill said. "What were you doing there?"

"Just before you were supposed to come over and study," Nick said, "someone knocked on the front door. When I opened it, no one was there. Instead there was a note. It was addressed to me, and it said to come to the house on Fear Street for some real action."

"Who was it from?"

"It wasn't signed," said Nick. "And then about five minutes later, Max came over. Someone had left the exact same note at his house. We both thought it was so weird we decided to check it out right away."

"You should have waited for me," said Jill.

"Then you'd be in trouble too," said Nick gloomily. "To be honest, the note was so strange I forgot all about our study date." He sighed. "This is terrible. I don't know what to do."

"Don't do anything yet," said Jill. "I'm going to talk to the others. Maybe we can get together and figure out what is going on."

"I hope so," said Nick. "Are you sure you heard the TV story right?"

"I'm sure," said Jill. "Talk to you later."

After putting down the receiver, she sat very still for several minutes. If Nick was telling the truth, and she thought he was, then someone else had set the fire.

The only one it could be was Gabe.

He must be completely out of control now, Jill thought. She should have realized that he would do something drastic after his father's car was set on fire.

She remembered how he vowed to get revenge on

the person who had set the car fire. How twisted and angry his face was. It *had* to be him.

Yet, a part of her didn't want to believe it. Didn't want to believe that Gabe was vengeful. Didn't want to believe he was a murderer, even if only by accident.

There must be another answer, she thought. And the only way she was going to find it was to talk to the others—separately or together. Talk to them all and find out what was going on.

Her mind made up, she picked up the receiver again and punched in Andrea's number. The line was busy. She waited a few minutes, then hit the Redial button, but Andrea's line was still tied up. Not wanting to wait any longer, she punched in Diane's number. Diane picked up on the third ring.

"Hello?"

"Diane, it's Jill," she said. "Do you have a minute?"

"Sure," said Diane. "What's wrong? You sound upset."

"I am upset," she admitted. "Something terrible has happened—and our friends are right in the middle of it."

"What?" Diane sounded alarmed.

"There was a fire on Fear Street tonight," Jill told her.

"Yes, I saw it on the news." Diane suddenly gasped. "It's not—it wasn't set by—" She didn't finish the thought.

But Jill understood what she was going to say. "I'm afraid it was. Nick and Max were there. Nick says they didn't set the fire but that someone sent them a note telling them to go there."

"Oh, Jill, how could he tell such an obvious lie?"

"I'm not sure he's lying," said Jill. "I've known him a long time. If it wasn't them, then it had to be Gabe."

"Oh, no," said Diane. "It couldn't have been him. I mean, I just can't believe he'd do such a thing."

"I never would have believed Nick would set someone's car on fire either," said Jill. "It's the whole fire game. It's made them all act crazy."

"I knew it!" said Diane, her voice trembling. "I knew it was wrong from the very beginning. Jill, we have to make them stop. We have to stop them *now.*"

"Yes, of course," said Jill.

"I mean *now,*" Diane repeated. "If we wait even one more day, who knows what might happen? Listen, my mom's asleep. I'll take her car and pick you up in about ten minutes."

"Where are we going?"

"Over to Nick's," said Diane. "We've got to talk to him, Jill. After Nick, we'll go see Max."

"But—"

"Really," Diane went on, "this is the best thing. You wouldn't be able to sleep now anyway, would you?"

"Well, no," Jill admitted.

"I'll be there in ten minutes," said Diane and hung up.

I feel as if I'm in a dream, Jill thought. It was getting late, and she was lightheaded from lack of sleep. This can't be happening, she told herself. I can't be involved in arson—and murder.

But as soon as she saw the brown station wagon in Nick's driveway, everything that had happened earlier came flooding back into her mind, and she realized that she *was* involved. They *all* were.

To her surprise, Max opened the door. "Nick called me as soon as he talked to you," he told Jill. "What are we going to do?"

"First we have to find out who set the fire," said Diane. "Did you do it?"

"Of course not!" said Max.

"I already explained what happened," said Nick, coming in from the other room.

"Jill said you got a note," Diane said. She sounded like a lawyer on TV.

"Yeah, we wouldn't make something like that up," said Max, annoyed. "Nick, have you still got yours?"

"I think so," said Nick. He went to his room, then came back holding a crumpled piece of paper.

He handed it to Jill. She held it so Diane could read it too. It said exactly what Nick had reported. But what he hadn't told her—and what she and Diane noticed at once—was that it was printed by a computer.

In blue ink.

chapter
17

Neither girl said a word. They just looked at each other, both thinking the same thing.

"Well?" said Max. "Do you believe us now? Or do you think that we wrote it ourselves?"

"We don't think you wrote it," said Jill sadly.

"I didn't mean to sound so suspicious," Diane added. "But after all, Jill saw you at the house on Fear Street."

"Yeah, well, someone else was there too," said Nick. "And whoever that person was set the fire."

"Did you see anyone?" Diane asked.

"No," said Nick. "The house seemed to be completely empty. We just hung around for a few minutes, and then there was this sort of thumping sound and the fire started. We ran away as fast as we could."

"Well, thanks for showing us the note," said Jill. "I guess we'd better go now."

"But I thought you wanted to talk the whole thing over," said Max. "I thought that was why you came here."

"Well, we did," said Jill, "but it's late, and we're all tired. Maybe it'll be better if we just sleep on it."

"All right," said Nick, but he looked at her as if she were crazy.

"It was Andrea's computer," Diane said in a shaky voice once they were back in her car.

"I know it," said Jill. "Unless—"

"Unless what?" said Diane. "Unless there's someone else in Shadyside with a blue-ink cartridge who knows all about the fire game?"

"I just can't believe she did it," said Jill.

"Me either," said Diane. "Or I don't want to. Andrea's a little wild sometimes, but she's basically okay. Maybe there's some other explanation."

"There must be," Jill agreed.

"You don't still think it was Gabe, do you?" said Diane. "You don't think Gabe *and* Andrea—"

"I don't know what to think," Jill answered.

"All I know is I want to hear what Andrea has to say about it," said Diane.

"Diane, it's awfully late," Jill objected.

"So what? Andrea always stays up late. Besides, we're only a couple of blocks from her house."

Jill nodded wearily. She was exhausted, but like Diane she did want to hear Andrea's explanation—if she had one.

"Well, hi, guys," said Andrea with a bright smile. She was wearing green-striped shorty pajamas but was wide-awake.

Jill sat on her bed, feeling terrible. Her eyes strayed to Andrea's desk and the computer. *How are we going*

94

to do this? she wondered. Should we just come out and—

But her thought was interrupted by Diane, who surprised her by coming right to the point. "We were just over at Nick's house," Diane said.

"What is this—your night to go visiting?" Andrea laughed. "Listen, if you want, I can throw some popcorn in the microwave."

"We didn't come here to hang out," Jill said. "We came to talk about something. Something very serious."

Andrea frowned, puzzled. Is she faking? Jill wondered. If so, she's very, very convincing.

"Nick showed us the note you sent him," Diane said then.

"What note?"

"The same one you sent Max," Diane went on.

"What are you talking about?" asked Andrea. "Why would I send them notes?"

"Andrea, we know you sent them. They were printed in blue ink."

"So what?" said Andrea, starting to sound annoyed. "What were these notes about?"

"They told the boys to go to a certain house on Fear Street for some real action."

"What?" Now Andrea started laughing. "Is this a late April Fools' joke, or what?"

"It's not a joke," Jill told her. And then, quickly, she told Andrea what she had heard on the late-night news.

Andrea listened until Jill finished explaining what Nick and Max had said. Then Andrea's expression changed to anger. "Let me get this straight," she said.

"You're saying that there was a fire over on Fear Street that killed a man, and that you think *I* set that fire?"

"It's just a possibility," said Jill quickly. "We're not accusing you of anything."

"Well, you're doing a pretty good imitation!" Andrea snapped. "Do you really think that I'd set a house on fire? And try to make it look like some of my friends had done it?"

Jill didn't answer. She really didn't think Andrea would do such a thing—except that everything pointed to her. How can this be happening? she thought.

"We don't want to believe it," Diane said, sounding more distressed than ever. "We thought maybe you could explain about the notes—"

"For your information, I don't have to explain anything to anybody!" said Andrea, her face red. "I thought you two were my friends!"

"We are," said Jill. "That's why we're here, instead—"

"Instead of what?" asked Andrea. "Instead of at the police station, turning me in for something you think I did?"

"Andrea, please," Jill begged. "Don't think that. We only—"

"Forget it," Andrea said. "I know what's really behind this. You're jealous of me because your date with Gabe was such a disaster! You're trying to get me in trouble so I won't go out with him!"

"That's not true!" said Jill.

"And somehow," Andrea went on, "you got Diane to go along with your little game! Well, forget it! I'll go out with anyone I want!"

"This isn't about Gabe, Andrea!" cried Diane. "I

didn't even know he and Jill had gone out. We're here because of what happened on Fear Street tonight. And because of the notes."

"What do you want?" Andrea snapped. "A full confession? Well, you won't get one, because I didn't write any notes and I didn't do anything else wrong!"

"All we want to do is stop the fires," Diane went on, her voice trembling. "And we want you to know that we're your friends and we'll stand by you no matter what."

"Some friends!" said Andrea. "Just go away and leave me alone!"

"Andrea, please—" said Jill.

"Get out!" Andrea screamed. "Didn't you hear me? This is my house and I don't want you in here! Not now—and not ever again!"

Andrea's face was so distorted with anger that Jill felt she hardly knew her.

She didn't want to believe that Andrea had set the fire.

But she *did* believe it. And from the look on Diane's face, she knew Diane believed it too.

chapter

18

*J*ill was startled out of a deep sleep by the jangling of her bedside phone. It took her a moment to realize she was awake. Then she picked up the receiver and managed a croaky "Hello?"

"Jill?" The voice spoke in a whisper, but Jill had no trouble recognizing it.

"Andrea?"

"Listen," Andrea said, "I'm sorry to call so late."

"That's okay. I had to get up to answer the phone anyway. What time is it?"

"Quarter past three," said Andrea. "But this is serious. Jill, I haven't been able to sleep a wink all night. I keep thinking about what you and Diane said when you came over."

Now the whole evening came rushing back to Jill, and she knew that she was back in the nightmare of the fire game. "Look, Andrea," she said, "we weren't trying to make you feel bad. It's just that we're both so worried about the fire."

"So you accused me of setting it!" Andrea said, her voice sounding teary.

"We didn't mean to accuse you of anything. We were just trying to find out what's going on!"

"I just want you to know," said Andrea, her voice again under control, "that I didn't have anything to do with the fire. But—but I've been thinking, and I have some ideas."

"About the fire?"

"I think I've got it figured out," she went on.

"You mean who set the fire?"

"And why," Andrea agreed.

"Tell me!" said Jill.

"Not tonight," said Andrea. "I need to do some more thinking. Can you get up early and meet me in the gym before classes tomorrow?"

"Sure," said Jill. "But why can't you—"

"Tomorrow," said Andrea. "But I will tell you this. I'm sure that it has to do with Gabe!"

Jill walked briskly in the bright spring sunshine, glad for the time alone. Usually her father gave her a ride to school on the way to work, but she had left much too early. As she walked, she kept going over Andrea's middle-of-the-night phone call and wondering what it might mean.

The night before, when Jill and Diane had gone over to Andrea's house, Andrea had sounded genuinely angry and upset about their suspicions. And over the phone she had still denied setting any fires.

But would someone who was really innocent get so upset over suspicions? Wouldn't she just laugh them off?

And what did Andrea mean that she had figured it all out? How? How could she have figured out anything unless she had been in on the fire or set it herself?

And most disturbing of all—what did she mean that it had to do with Gabe?

The night before, Andrea had accused Jill of being jealous because her date with Gabe had gone badly. But Jill suspected that the opposite might be true— that Andrea was jealous of Jill, because Gabe had asked her out first.

Was that why she was accusing Gabe of setting the fires?

But wait, Jill thought. Andrea hadn't accused Gabe of anything—she had just said that the fire had to do with him.

What could it all mean?

By the time Jill reached school, she was more confused than ever.

She wasn't used to being at school so early. There were only a few cars in the teachers' parking lot and none at all in the students' lot. The flower beds along the front walk were full of daffodil buds, their yellow tips showing the promise of flowers just about to bloom. At the end of the driveway, Mr. Peterson, the head custodian, was hosing off the sidewalk. No one else was in view.

Jill knew that Andrea often came to school early to practice gymnastics. Andrea said she liked it because it was peaceful and she didn't have to worry about anyone watching her. She did it so often that she had her own key to the gym.

Jill went up the familiar front steps into the main

hall. Her footsteps echoed in the quiet as she walked toward the gym.

The door was open a crack, and she slipped into the huge wood-paneled gym. The lights weren't on, but enough sunlight filtered through the windows to show all the equipment in relief. At first glance the room seemed empty.

"Andrea?" she called. "Andrea, I'm here."

There was no answer. She looked around more carefully, but obviously no one was there.

Frowning, Jill crossed the polished wooden floor toward the girls' locker room. Maybe she overslept, she thought. After all, when Andrea had called, she'd said that she hadn't been able to sleep a wink the whole night.

Or maybe, Jill suddenly thought, this is just a practical joke, to get back at me for what Diane and I said last night. Or maybe Andrea was talking in her sleep, or maybe she's in the locker room.

She opened the blue door and stepped into the locker room. Even empty, it held the familiar scent of sneakers, dirty socks, and sweaty bodies. "Andrea?" she called. "Andrea, are you in here?"

"Jill?" a voice called to her from the far corner, where the stalls were.

"Diane?" Jill was startled.

"Hi," said Diane, putting down a magazine. She was wearing one of her long-sleeved leotards, this one a brilliant blue that matched her eyes.

"What are you doing here?" Jill asked.

"I could ask you the same thing," said Diane. "I got a call from Andrea in the middle of the night. She said she was sorry she blew up at me and asked if I'd come spot her this morning while she practiced her routine."

"You're kidding," said Jill.

"I thought it was a little strange," Diane admitted. "Especially since she called so late. But I thought maybe it would be a good way of getting her to talk about—well, you know."

"So where is she?" asked Jill.

"Home asleep is my guess," said Diane. "She asked me to be here at six-thirty. So I've been waiting around ever since, but no Andrea."

"She called me too," said Jill. "Do you suppose this is just a trick to get even with us for last night?"

"Maybe," said Diane doubtfully. "But it doesn't seem like something Andrea would do. Besides, we didn't really do anything to her last night. We were just trying to help."

"Except she didn't see it that way," said Jill. She frowned, as she glanced around. "I guess she must have just—wait a minute."

"What?" Diane followed Jill's gaze to the locker area.

"She *is* here," said Jill. "Look—her locker's empty."

The girls went over to the locker bank. And sure enough, Andrea's lock was missing from her locker, which was open and empty. A lock—presumably Andrea's—hung on the nearest large wardrobe locker.

"So she *is* here," Diane said. "Maybe she's out jogging. Sometimes she does that for a warm-up."

"I don't think so," said Jill. "I was just outside. Let's go back to the gym. Maybe she just stepped out for a minute."

The two friends went back into the gymnasium,

half expecting to see Andrea practicing on the mat. The big room was still empty.

"Well, she's here somewhere," said Diane. "We might as well just wait."

"Right," said Jill. "I think I'll practice a little while we do." She walked over to the tumbling mat and warmed up with a couple of cartwheels. She was about to practice a forward roll when she saw something that didn't belong next to the balance beam.

Something red and crumpled.

"Diane!" she called, her heart going to her throat.

Both girls ran over to the beam. The flash of red that Jill had seen was Andrea's leotard.

Lying just to the side of the balance beam, her arms twisted under her, was Andrea, her body motionless, her face white as paste.

"I don't believe it!" Diane cried. "She's dead!"

chapter
19

"Andrea!" Jill felt as if her own heart had stopped beating. "Andrea!"

Her friend didn't move or respond in any way. The faint outline of a blue bruise was beginning to form on her pale forehead.

"She's—dead?" Diane repeated, her voice a frightened whisper.

"I don't know," said Jill. She placed her head to her friend's chest and relaxed when she heard the even, steady beating of Andrea's heart. "I hear her heart," she said with relief. "And she's—she's breathing."

"Thank God!" cried Diane. "Don't move her. I'll go call an ambulance."

The wail of the siren died away in the distance, and Jill sat shakily on one of the benches in the locker room. Looking totally drained, Diane slumped down next to her.

"She's going to be okay," Jill said. "She's got to be."

"She was so pale," Diane said breathily. "And that bruise—"

"I know," said Jill.

The ambulance had come almost immediately. A few minutes later, the gym had been filled with people—paramedics, police officers, the principal, and eventually Miss Mercer, the gymnastics coach. All of them had wanted to know what had happened. But neither Diane nor Jill could tell them more than that Andrea had asked them both to meet her before school.

Because of the bruise on her forehead, and because of where Andrea had been found, everyone assumed that she must have lost her balance and fallen off the beam.

"How could she have done such a stupid thing?" Diane asked, echoing Jill's thought for the hundredth time. "I told her I'd be here to spot her. Why couldn't she have waited for me?"

"It doesn't make any sense," said Jill. "Even Miss Mercer agrees. Andrea is simply too experienced to try a difficult routine without a spotter."

"Unless maybe she wanted to fall," said Diane.

"What?"

"I don't mean consciously," said Diane. "But maybe deep inside, Andrea felt guilty about the fire. Maybe this was some sort of unconscious way for her to punish herself."

"That's too deep for me," said Jill. "Andrea's not like that, and you know she isn't. She's the most straightforward person we know."

"Guilt does strange things to people," Diane said. "It can muddle their thinking, Jill. It can make them do things they wouldn't ordinarily do."

"Maybe," said Jill. "But I—I don't believe it. In fact, I'm not sure that Andrea's fall was an accident."

"What do you mean?" Diane asked, her blue eyes suddenly wide with horror.

"I don't know," Jill said. Almost as if they had been spoken inside her head, she remembered again Andrea's words that the fires had to do with Gabe. If she had been right, and Gabe knew that Andrea suspected him . . .

It was almost too horrible to consider, but could Gabe have had something to do with Andrea's "accident"?

"I don't know," Jill repeated. "But I mean to find out."

"You're probably wondering why I called this meeting," cracked Max, standing at the front of the room.

"Sit down, you nerd," said Nick. "Anyway, you didn't call it. Jill did. And, to tell the truth, I am wondering why."

"I think it's obvious," said Jill. She was sitting in an overstuffed tweed chair in the TV room at Diane's house. Once she had figured out what she had to do and explained it to Diane, it had been easy to set in motion. She had spoken to Nick and Max, and Diane had asked Gabe. Gabe, the last to arrive, was now sitting on the rug in front of the fireplace, a sarcastic smile on his face.

Diane sat across from him, in an easy chair, her eyes big, serious, and sad looking, while Max and Nick both slouched on the leather sofa.

Jill had expected to feel nervous, but instead she felt very much in control.

At last we're going to find out what's going on, she

thought. She cleared her throat and continued. "It's obvious why we're here. All of you know what happened to Andrea this morning, and I thought we should get together to talk about it and discuss everything that's happened."

"Discuss who set the fire, you mean," said Nick, already sounding angry.

"That's part of it," said Jill. "But also discuss what happened to Andrea—and why."

"Who knows why someone has an accident?" said Max. "I feel really bad for Andrea, but I don't see what it has to do with the fire."

"It might have *everything* to do with it," said Diane. "Especially if Andrea is the one who set the Fear Street fire." Quickly she explained about the blue ribbon in Andrea's printer. "Jill and I know she did it," Diane went on. "And she knows we know. What if her guilt got to be too much, and . . ." She let the thought trail off.

"And she jumped off the balance beam deliberately?" asked Max, his face full of disbelief. "Tell us another one, Diane."

"I don't know," said Nick. "It makes a little sense, except I can't believe Andrea was the one who set the fire."

"What about the notes?" said Diane.

"I'm sure there's more than one person in Shadyside with a blue printer ribbon," said Nick. "Besides, what reason would she have? The competition to set fires was between us guys."

"So you're saying one of you did it?" said Jill.

"I think it's obvious," said Nick. "Just as it's obvious which one it was." He directed his gaze at Gabe, and Gabe returned the look casually.

"Are you accusing me?" Gabe challenged.

"Hey, man," said Nick. "You're the one who's in love with fire. The rest of us just went along with it."

"Is that what you believe?" said Gabe. He was still smiling, but it wasn't a friendly smile, and his voice had acquired a hard edge that Jill found frightening.

"It had to be Andrea!" Diane protested quickly. "She was into the fire game from the beginning. And in spite of what Nick says, we know that she has a blue printer ribbon."

"We can't be sure Andrea wrote the notes," said Jill. "In fact, we can't be sure of anything. But now that something has happened to Andrea, I think our trouble is only beginning."

"What are you talking about?" said Nick.

"I mean—what if it wasn't one of us? What if it was someone else, someone who found out about the fire game and knows that the fire department is investigating?"

"What do you think this is—a James Bond movie?" asked Gabe.

"I'm serious," Jill protested. She hadn't actually considered it before, but now that she was talking about it, she realized that this had been in the back of her mind all day. "Anyone could have found out about the fire game. And what if that person wants to use it against us? Blackmail us or threaten us in some way? And what if they first went to Andrea . . ."

"Pathetic," said Gabe.

Jill realized he was speaking to her, and she was suddenly filled with a sick anger. "What's pathetic?" she demanded furiously.

"You. All of you. Your complicated plots. Trying to explain something that's actually very simple."

"Oh, really?" Jill said. "If it's so simple, suppose you explain it to us." She was so angry that her voice was shaking, and for a moment she thought Gabe looked hurt. Then his face changed, and once again he was smiling that infuriating, superior smile.

"Face it, Jill," he said, shrugging. "All of you enjoyed the fire game—even you, Di. It gave you a few moments of excitement for the first time in years—maybe the first time ever. You even got to read about yourselves in the paper."

"So what?" said Jill.

"So nothing," said Gabe. "There's no mysterious stranger who wants to blackmail us. There's no one mysterious at all. The Fear Street fire, the notes—it's obvious who did it. It had to be one of us."

chapter
_____
20

A sudden spring wind had come up, and Jill kept her head down against the chill. It was as dark as the inside of a cave, and she began to imagine she saw shapes moving in every shadow.

Maybe she should have accepted Gabe's offer of a ride home. But then she remembered his smug, sarcastic look when he'd said her idea was "pathetic."

Right after Gabe had said one of the group must have set the fire, the meeting had completely broken down, with everyone accusing everyone else. Nick was so angry that his usually pale face had turned red. And no one had taken Jill's idea seriously that it might have been someone outside the group. Someone who wanted to get the friends in trouble—or worse.

But what if it *was* some stranger? Jill thought. What would that person possibly want with them?

A car turned the far corner of the street and began to slow down as it approached her.

Why had she decided to walk? It was still nearly six

blocks to her house. The car was barely rolling now as it drew nearer. She sneaked a glance back. A white Taurus. She had never seen the car before in her life.

Her heart pounding furiously, Jill began to walk faster, staring straight ahead. She heard the car pull alongside her and continue to roll, at the same pace she was walking.

Wildly, Jill glanced around. There was a house just ahead with its lights on. She started to turn into the walk, pretending she lived there, and then the car stopped. The engine cut off and the door slammed.

Not even thinking, Jill ran up the walk, then stumbled, sprawling on the front porch. She heard steps coming up the walk behind her.

Nearly frozen in terror, she opened her mouth to scream.

"Hey, Jill!"

"No!" she cried.

"Jill! Hey, Jill! It's me!"

She looked up and nearly melted with relief. It was Gabe, his expression a mixture of confusion and amusement. "Who did you think I was?" he said. "One of the undead?"

"Gabe!" she said. "I—I didn't recognize your car."

"It's the rental my dad just got," he said. He held out a hand and pulled her to her feet, then led her to the car.

"Come on, get in," he said.

"Okay," she said in a small voice. "Thanks." She climbed into the front seat beside him. He was looking at her almost tenderly, the way he had on their date. It had been only Saturday, but so much had happened, it seemed like years ago.

Gabe didn't start the car again. He kept looking at her, his handsome face very serious but also very kind.

"I'm sorry for what I said before," he said. "I didn't mean to come down so hard on you." She didn't know what to answer. "Jill?"

"You didn't even listen to my idea," she said. "You just said it was pathetic."

"Bad choice of words," Gabe said. "But your idea seems a little unlikely, don't you think?"

"No," said Jill. "I don't think so. I mean, I can't believe any one of us could have done such a terrible thing." Any one of us, but you, she thought.

"You mean you don't *want* to believe it," said Gabe. "You don't want to face the fact that one of your very best friends might be an arsonist or worse. Isn't that right?"

"Of course I don't want to believe it!" said Jill.

"So it's easier to think that it's some mysterious stranger," Gabe said. "I can get behind that. No one wants to believe something bad about someone they care about." He said it so seriously that Jill had a sudden eerie feeling that he knew more than he was telling.

"Who do you think it was?" she whispered.

"I don't want to make an accusation," he said. "Not now."

Jill couldn't think what to say.

After a moment Gabe sighed and started the car up again. "I'd better get you home," he said.

He drove in silence for a moment, then said, almost to himself, "It would be better if I'd never come here."

"Don't say that," said Jill.

"Why?" He almost smiled. "Are you glad I'm here?"

"You know I am," she said. "But—but I'm not glad about some of the things that have happened."

"Neither am I," Gabe said, again serious. "I should have known better."

"What do you mean?"

"Never mind," he said. "But, Jill, I think the best thing for you to do is forget all about that fire on Fear Street. I have a feeling the fires are over. If you keep investigating, you might find out that you're *really* playing with fire, in more ways than one."

Is that a warning? she wondered. Or a threat? She looked over at him as he drove, his clear green eyes fixed on the road. There was a strange expression on his face—almost sad. What's he trying to tell me? she wondered. That he set the fire himself and he's not going to do it anymore?

Gabe pulled the car into Jill's driveway and cut the engine. "I'll walk you to the door," he said. "I can manage to be a true gentleman about two or three times a year."

He came around and opened her door, then gently put his arm around her as he walked her to the porch. Once again Jill felt herself melting. If only she could trust him!

At her door he leaned down and kissed her on the cheek. "This has all gotten too heavy," he said. "What do you say we forget about fires and accusations and catch a movie Friday—tomorrow night?"

"I—I don't know," said Jill.

"You don't know if you're free, or you don't know if you want to go out with me?" There was no trace of his sarcastic smile, only a look of gentleness.

"I guess," said Jill, "I'm wondering if you really want to go out with *me*."

Gabe understood. "Because of Andrea?" She nodded. "I like her a lot, Jill. And I'm hoping she recovers from her accident soon. But the other night was—just one of those things. She was all over me—what could I do?"

"I just wanted to make sure," she said, "that there wasn't something more going on."

"Does this mean we're on for Friday night?"

"Sure," said Jill. "Why not?"

"Good," he said. He kissed her again, this time on the lips, then waited while she opened the door. "See you later," he said.

Jill shut the door and leaned against it, her heart pounding. Oh, Gabe, she thought, what am I going to do about you?

The real question, of course, was, what was she going to do about her feelings for him?

She went into the family room and found Mittsy curled up on the sofa, the TV playing softly in the background. She switched it off. Her parents were out playing bridge with some friends, and the house felt empty.

She sat petting the cat, staring at the TV without seeing it, and thinking about Andrea, Gabe, and the fires. But mostly she was thinking about Gabe.

Maybe he was right, that the best thing for her to do was just forget about the Fear Street fire. Even if he set it—or knew who did—he seemed to be telling her that there wouldn't be any more fires.

She stretched, then decided to work on her algebra homework. She was just heading up the stairs when the doorbell rang.

Maybe it's Gabe, she thought. She pulled open the door and was surprised to see two men in suits standing there. "I'm Detective Frazier," the taller one told her, holding out his ID. "This is my partner, Detective Monroe. Are you Jill Franks?"

"Yes," she said.

"Do you mind if we come in? We want to ask you some questions about a fire on Fear Street."

chapter

21

"Come on in," she said, hoping that her voice wasn't shaking.

Be casual, she told herself. You haven't done anything wrong.

"We're sorry to bother you at this hour," said Detective Frazier. "Can you tell us where you were last night, the twentieth?"

"Last night? I was out driving around," Jill said.

"Yes?" said Frazier. He seemed friendly and not at all suspicious. "Our records indicate that one of our officers saw you on Fear Street last night just before a fire killed a homeless man. He said you had some sort of car trouble."

"That's right," said Jill. "My car stalled out."

"Do you mind telling us what you were doing on Fear Street?" asked Detective Monroe.

Jill thought fast. "I—I had a fight with my boyfriend. I didn't want to be home if he called. So I thought I'd just drive around. I didn't realize I was on Fear Street until my car stalled."

Detective Frazier raised one eyebrow.

"While you were on Fear Street, did you see anything suspicious?"

"I didn't see anything at all," Jill said. "I was too busy trying to start my car." She was amazed at how easily the lies came to her. But what else could she do? She was almost certain that Max and Nick hadn't started the fire, and if she told about them they would be in terrible trouble.

But what if they *did* start the fire? Another part of her wanted to tell the policemen everything, to get it all out in the open.

"You didn't see any other people?" asked Monroe. "Did you see the fire?"

"No, really, Officer," she said. "I didn't see anything."

"Our records indicate that the fire was called in from a fire box at the corner of Old Mill Road and Fear Street around the time you were there," he said.

"It must have been someone else," said Jill. She looked at both detectives intently, but their faces seemed relaxed and free of suspicion.

"Well, I guess that's about it," said Frazier cheerfully, closing his notebook. "We won't take up any more of your time."

They don't suspect me, Jill thought with relief.

"If you think of anything that might help our investigation," Detective Monroe added, "please get in touch." He handed Jill a card with his number on it, and then both men lumbered out the door. They were about to start down the front steps when Detective Frazier suddenly turned. "By the way," he said, and this time his face was not friendly, "if we need you, we know where you are."

chapter
22

*J*ill peered through the living room curtain until the officers had driven away, then, feeling shaken, went to her room and got ready for bed. She felt sad, guilty, and on the verge of tears.

What I did was wrong, she told herself. Lying to the police is a crime.

But what else could I have done? she wondered. If she'd told about Max and Nick, they would have been prime suspects. And she was sure they hadn't set the fire. Even worse, the whole thing about the fire game would have come out, including the computer notes, and Andrea was already in enough trouble.

Thinking about Andrea made her feel even worse. Had her fall really been an accident? If not, what had happened, and who was responsible?

She punched in the hospital number and asked for patient information. "Andrea Hubbard," she said. "She was admitted this morning. I just wondered how she was doing."

There was silence while the woman on the other end

looked through her records. "There's no change," she reported at last.

Jill thanked her and hung up. No change. That meant that Andrea was still unconscious. She remembered how pale and broken Andrea had looked that morning. What if she never woke up?

Suddenly Jill realized that she couldn't go on lying. That none of them could. The police might not suspect her now, but they knew that she had been on Fear Street that night. Someone might have seen Nick's father's car as well.

There was only one answer. They—all of them— had to go to the police and tell what they knew. With a great feeling of relief, Jill punched in Diane's number.

Diane, sympathetic as ever, listened to Jill seriously. "You say the police didn't suspect you?" she asked.

"No," said Jill. "But it doesn't matter. I just realized this whole thing has gone too far. We have to tell what we know. I want you to help me convince the guys."

"That's not going to be easy," Diane said doubtfully. "I mean, Nick and Max were there when the fire started."

"But they said they didn't do it and I believe them," said Jill. "The one who's going to be hard to convince is Gabe. He told me I should just forget about the whole thing. That he doesn't think there'll be any more fires."

"When did he tell you that?" said Diane.

"After the meeting," said Jill. "He picked me up while I was walking home."

"That's a surprise," said Diane. "By the end of the meeting you two weren't even speaking."

"I know," said Jill. "No offense, since he's your

friend, but Gabe is strange. First he was talking really seriously about the fire, and about five minutes later he completely cheered up and asked me out."

"Really?" said Diane. "You're not going, are you?"

"I said I would," said Jill. "But after the police came over, I don't know. I don't know if I want to go out with anyone until this whole thing is resolved."

"I think you're right," said Diane. "Gabe's always been terribly moody, and—"

"That's what I was thinking," Jill said.

"I have an idea," said Diane. "Why not just forget about Gabe and all the others? You and I can go to my parents' cabin this weekend. Just get away from everything."

"That sounds great," said Jill. "But what about the police?"

"I agree we should tell them what we know," said Diane. "But, Jill, you're too upset to think straight now. If we go to the cabin, we'll have time to figure out what to tell them. Besides, maybe by the time we get back, they'll have found the person responsible and we won't have to say anything."

Jill thought a moment. It would only be for a couple of days. And Diane was right—she *was* too upset to think straight. Gabe might be angry that she was breaking the date—but the way she felt now, she didn't see how she could just go out and act as if nothing had happened.

"You're on for the weekend," she told her friend. "In fact, it sounds like just what I need."

chapter

23

"This was the best idea, Diane!" Jill leaned against the cushions and stretched her legs out toward the fireplace. "It was great of your folks to let us have the cabin."

"My dad had to work this weekend, so they weren't going to use it anyway," said Diane.

"Some of his sculptures are pretty wild," said Jill, admiring the free-form metal sculptures that sat on nearly every flat surface. A small metal mobile hanging from the center of the room swayed noisily with every breeze.

"That one's my favorite," said Diane, following the direction of Jill's gaze. "Dad said he'll give it to me when I have a place of my own someday." She stretched and yawned. "Want more pizza?"

"I'm stuffed," said Jill. Instead of cooking out, they'd microwaved frozen pizzas.

"Me too," said Diane.

"It's so nice here, so peaceful," said Jill.

"I told you we'd be able to relax this weekend,"

Diane agreed. "What did Gabe say when you broke your date with him for tonight?"

"He didn't get mad or anything," said Jill, still feeling strange about the conversation. "I told him my parents wanted me to stay in. He said he understood. You know, he can be nice sometimes."

"I know," said Diane.

"And at other times he's so wild. If it weren't for him, there would never have been any fires."

"He's always been that way," said Diane. "Always wanting to do something different, even if it's crazy."

"Somehow," Jill went on, "I can't help feeling that Gabe's the key to the whole thing—even if he didn't set the fire on Fear Street. We've got to talk to him, Diane. As soon as we get back home."

"We will," said Diane, "but for now, let's just forget everything and take it easy."

"But I thought we agreed we'd figure out what to do about the fires this weekend," Jill pressed.

"Don't worry," said Diane. "We will. But we don't have to talk about it every single minute." She yawned again. "I'm going to go take a shower now. You want the bathroom first?"

"No, thanks. I think I'll just sit here and read for a while." Jill picked up a historical novel she'd been reading. After a few minutes she realized she'd read the same page over and over.

It's no good, she thought, putting the book down. I'm not going to be able to concentrate on anything till we get the whole thing about the fire settled once and for all. Diane didn't seem to want to talk about it, and Jill couldn't blame her. It had been on all their minds too much. But it would be better to talk it out and get it over with.

As soon as Diane gets out of the shower, Jill thought, I'm going to insist—

Her thought was broken by the ringing of the telephone. It took Jill a moment to find it, on a bench with Diane's father's sculpting tools.

"Hello?" she said.

"Hi," said a wonderfully familiar voice.

"Andrea!" cried Jill. "How are you?"

"Recovering," said Andrea. "The doctors say I'm going to be fine. Sort of blows your little plan to pieces, doesn't it?"

"What are you talking about?" said Jill. "I'm so happy you're all right!"

"I'll bet you are," said Andrea. "But you can quit pretending. I know it was you. When you didn't show up, I started warming up on the beam—probably just as you thought I would. The next thing I knew someone hit me from behind. It had to be you."

Jill felt a jolt of fear run down her spine. "Andrea," she said carefully, "you're not making any sense. You've had a bad head injury. Maybe you ought to get a good night's sleep and we can talk in the morning."

Andrea laughed. "I may have a head injury," she said, "but I don't have amnesia. And I've had a lot of time to think. I know you printed the notes too, the day you came over to my house. I know everything, Diane."

"Diane?" gasped Jill. "Andrea—this is me, Jill."

"Jill!" Andrea sounded shocked. "I—I didn't recognize your voice. I didn't know you were there."

"Diane invited me to spend the weekend," Jill said. "But what did you mean about—"

"Jill, listen to me," said Andrea urgently. "You've got to get out of there right away! Diane's dangerous! I think she's the one who set the fire. I know she hit me over the head—"

"But, Andrea, that doesn't make any sense! Diane's terrified of fires, and why would she want to hurt you?"

"To keep me away from Gabe!" said Andrea. "She's in love with him, Jill, and she's crazy!"

Gabe! With a sinking feeling, Jill began to understand. "But, Andrea," she protested, "if what you say is true, Diane needs help."

"Of course she does!" said Andrea. "That's what I was going to tell her. I—I was even going to offer to help her give herself up. But, Jill, we can talk about it later. She knows you're dating Gabe now. You've got to get out of there. Please! Do it now."

"But she invited me here so we could talk—"

"That's even worse! Please, Jill, please, just leave. Promise me you'll leave now. We can figure out what to do later."

Jill was about to protest again, but Andrea's urgency and fright were very real, and Jill began to feel a rising panic. If what Andrea said was true, that meant Diane was a murderer. And she had tried to kill Andrea. Now Jill was alone in the cabin with her.

"Okay, Andrea," she told her friend. "I'll leave now. I'll call you as soon as I get back home."

She quickly hung up the phone, then grabbed her overnight bag. She could still hear the water running in the bathroom. For a moment she considered telling Diane that she felt sick and was going home, but she remembered the urgency in Andrea's voice, so she slipped out the cabin door and shut it behind her.

Sliding into her car, she opened her purse and fished around for her keys. She usually kept them in the side zipper compartment. But there was nothing there but a lipstick and a small pack of tissues. Switching on the car light, she dumped the contents of her purse onto the bucket seat beside her.

No keys.

She shuffled through the clutter of stuff again.

No keys.

Had Diane taken them?

If so, it meant that she wanted to make sure Jill stayed there—maybe for good.

chapter
24

*J*ill felt cold, unreasoning fear move through her body. I've got to get out of here, she thought.

She slid out of the car and looked around frantically. A path led through the woods away from the lake. If she followed it, she was bound to come to a road or maybe even another cabin, one with a phone where she could call for help.

There was no moon, and the woods were dark and forbidding. She remembered hearing somewhere that the Fear Street woods were much darker than woods anywhere else.

She didn't even want to think about the other things she'd heard about the woods—such as the stories about the living dead who roamed through them at night. Or the fact that some people who had ventured into the woods had never been seen again.

At the edge of the path she forced herself to stop and take three deep breaths to calm down. She glanced back at the cabin and saw the bathroom light go out.

Diane knows I'm gone now, she realized. Without another thought she began to follow the path, straight into the dark thicket of trees and shrubs.

In a very short time, Jill found herself in total darkness. The light from Diane's cabin was a memory. She was walking as quickly as she could but had to be careful to stay on the path. "Ouch!" She walked into a thick bush.

Something yelped, then skittered off behind her.

A raccoon, she thought. Or maybe a bird.

She kept walking, more careful than ever to stay on the path. And then she became aware of a sound behind her. The sound of someone walking, of dry twigs breaking in a regular rhythm.

Someone's after me! she thought.

Or something.

Her heart was pounding so hard she could hardly breathe. Just ahead she saw a break in the trees. She deliberately stepped off the path, then froze behind a large oak, waiting for the thing that was stalking her to pass.

The sounds of footsteps continued, but she couldn't see anything. A moment later the sound faded away into the distance.

Maybe it was just the wind, she thought.

Maybe.

In any case, she didn't dare follow the path any longer. Instead, she struck out through the trees, trying to keep herself oriented away from the lake.

There's got to be a cabin out here, she thought. Lots of people have places in the woods.

But there was no sign of a light, only woods and more woods.

With sudden horror she realized she was no longer sure where the lake was, or even the path. It was so dark, she couldn't be sure what direction she had come from.

This can't be happening, she thought. I can't be out in the middle of the Fear Street woods, at night and alone. I can't be lost.

But she was.

She forced herself to stop and catch her breath. Maybe she could just wait here, where she was, until daylight.

Sure, Jill, she told herself. Just wait here in the dark with the living dead walking around and a murderer after you. She felt so frightened she wanted to laugh— or cry.

More slowly now she began to walk again, back toward the lake. She realized now that she should have done that in the first place. If she followed the lake around she would surely run into other cabins. There was even a little grocery store on the side of the lake across from Diane's parents' cabin.

That's it, she told herself. Find the lake.

She kept going in what she hoped was the right direction. After what seemed a very long time, but was probably only minutes, she saw a light in the distance.

The light was moving.

It's a flashlight! she thought. It's someone who can help me!

Weak with relief, she began to stumble toward the light.

"Hello!" she called. "I'm lost! Can you help me?"

"Of course I can," said the person holding the light. The figure stepped closer, and Jill felt her heart sink to the bottom of her feet.

It was Diane.

chapter

25

"What are you doing out here?" Diane asked, her blue eyes wide with surprise above the flashlight. "Jill, I was so worried about you." She was wearing a jacket over her robe, and her hair was still wrapped in a towel from the shower.

For a moment Jill couldn't think of a single thing to say.

How had Diane found her?

Diane answered, as if she had read her thoughts, "When I saw you weren't in the cabin, I thought—I don't know what I thought, but I was scared. Then I found your car keys lying on the porch."

"I was lost," Jill said, bewildered. "How did you find me?"

"I followed your footsteps," said Diane. "You walked in a circle. The cabin's right over there."

Jill turned to face where Diane was pointing. Sure enough, the glow from the cabin lights was visible through the trees.

"But what in the world are you doing out here?" Diane repeated. "It's not safe in the woods at night."

"I know," said Jill. "I just—just wanted to get some fresh air."

"Well, it's cold," said Diane. "Look at you, you're shivering. Here, take my jacket." She slipped out of her jacket and put it over Jill's shoulders. "Poor Jill, you must really be upset to do such a foolish thing. Come on back in the cabin. We can talk about it if you want."

Jill didn't know what to think. Diane seemed just like herself, always worried about other people. How could the things Andrea had accused her of be true?

On the other hand, the panic in Andrea's voice had been real.

But even if it was true, even if Diane had set the fire, what could Diane do to her? Jill was bigger than Diane, and if she had set the fires, maybe she did want to talk about it. Maybe if Jill just went inside and played it cool, she could find out what was going on.

The cabin was warm and cheery after the terrifying moments out in the woods, and Jill stood close to the fireplace, trying to get warm.

"I'll make some tea," said Diane. "It'll just take a minute. Why don't you wrap up in that blanket and sit close to the fire?"

Jill did as Diane suggested and sat by the hearth, shivering. She watched as Diane heated water, her pretty face lined with worry.

How could Diane have possibly done the things Andrea accused her of? she wondered. She's so sweet and so caring. Maybe Andrea's accident had somehow affected her mind.

"Thanks," Jill said as Diane brought her the tea.

"Just sip it slowly," said Diane. She sat on a worn leather ottoman across from Jill.

How am I going to bring up what I want to talk about? Jill wondered. But Diane saved her the trouble.

"I thought I heard the phone ring while I was in the shower," Diane said. "Who was it?"

Jill took a deep breath. "It was Andrea."

"Really?" said Diane, surprised. "But I thought she was still unconscious."

"She came out of it," said Jill. "She's going to be all right. But, Diane—she had some things to say that were really upsetting. Things about you."

"Me? What do you mean?" said Diane.

"I mean," said Jill, swallowing, "that Andrea thinks you were the one who wrote the notes."

"The notes?" said Diane. "You mean the ones printed in blue ink? Andrea thinks I did that?"

"Yes," said Jill.

"But that's ridiculous!" said Diane. "It was her computer—we all knew that."

"The only person who was so *sure* it was Andrea's computer was you," said Jill, suddenly realizing that was true. "The rest of us kept saying it could have been another computer with blue ink."

"Are you saying *you* think I wrote the notes?" said Diane. She sounded shocked.

"I don't know what I think," said Jill truthfully.

"What else did Andrea say?" Diane demanded.

"She said—she said you hit her from behind while she was practicing on the balance beam."

"She told you that," Diane repeated. It wasn't a question.

"Yes."

"And I suppose you believed her about that too?" said Diane. Her face had changed, and her expression was no longer sweet and concerned. She looked angry and determined. But determined about what?

"I told you," Jill said. "I don't know what I believe."

Diane sighed and then she smiled, very strangely. "All right, Jill, I guess it's time to tell you the truth. I *was* the one who wrote the notes. And, yes, I did hit Andrea."

"But why?" Jill was horrified.

"Why?" Diane laughed. "That's easy. Because she knew the truth! And now, I'm sorry to say, you know it too. . . ."

chapter

26

For a moment Jill just stared at Diane, shocked. Despite what Andrea had told her, in spite of Diane's own confession, she couldn't believe it.

Was this really her friend Diane? Sweet, considerate Diane, who only a few minutes ago had lovingly made her a cup of hot tea?

She almost didn't recognize the girl who sat across from her now, her usually sweet and pretty face transformed by a mocking, cruel smile.

Diane unwrapped the towel from around her head and shook her damp, curly hair loose.

"What's the matter, Jill?" she said. "Cat got your tongue?"

"I just—just can't believe it," Jill said.

"Oh, really?" said Diane. "Well, it's true. There are a lot of things you don't know, Jill. You live in such a dream world, with everything always going your way, with boys falling all over you. You think you can have any boy you want, don't you?"

"I never thought that."

"Didn't you?" said Diane. "What about Gabe?"

"I've only been out with him once," Jill said in a small voice, her feelings of shock beginning to give way to horror.

"But you had big plans for him, didn't you?" Diane went on. "Probably thought you could add him to your string, along with Nick and Max." Then, with sudden fury, she added, "But you can't have him!"

Jill continued to stare at Diane, sickened and horrified by the look of hatred she saw on her face. "You said yourself you didn't care about him," she protested. "You told Andrea he was only an old family friend."

"What was I supposed to say?" Diane sneered. "That I've loved him since I was a little girl? That there's no way Gabe and I can ever be together? A real friend would have figured it out!"

"Diane, I'm sorry." Jill spoke quickly, trying to get through to her friend. "I never meant to hurt you. I never would have dated Gabe if I'd known how you felt. And I promise—I promise I'll never see him again!"

"It's too late," Diane said coldly.

Jill felt a sudden chill. "What do you mean?"

"What do you think?" said Diane. "I mean you'll never have another chance." She paused, then went on, almost matter-of-factly. "For a while I thought you were different—not like Andrea. When I saw her kissing Gabe, I knew I had to get rid of her."

"But it was your idea for Gabe to write music for her routine."

"I didn't think it would go any further than that," Diane said.

"That's why you hit her?" Jill said.

"No!" Diane sounded annoyed. "I already told you I hit her because she found out that I was the one who framed her for the fire on Fear Street."

"You set the fire?" Jill asked, astonished.

"Fires," said Diane. "That's plural. I also set Gabe's car on fire."

"But why?" The things that Diane was telling Jill seemed crazier and crazier.

"I saw Gabe with a girl in the park that night," Diane told her. "He was singing to her—singing a song he wrote for me. I didn't know it was you. I thought it was Andrea, because of the way she was coming on to him."

"So you set his car on fire?" Jill asked in disbelief.

"I thought it might keep him from going out with her again," Diane said, sounding calm and reasonable. "Anyway, I didn't want him to see me, and then when I spotted his dad's car, it was easy. He never locks it."

"But how could you have done that? You're terrified of fire!"

Diane's expression changed again, to one of amusement. "That used to be true. But did you ever hear of a love-hate relationship? For a long time I thought fire was my enemy. But now that I know what it can do, fire is my friend."

She's crazy, Jill realized. How could I have known her all these months and not realized?

But maybe, she thought, maybe I helped to push her over the edge. If we hadn't all gotten into the fire game, maybe none of this would have happened.

"Diane," she said gently, again trying to break through to her friend. "I feel so sorry about all this.

And I can see that—that my being here is upsetting you. So if you'll just give me my car keys, I'll go on home and we can talk about all this next week."

"Go home?" said Diane. "Why should I let you go home? I planned this weekend, Jill. I got rid of Andrea, and now it's time to get rid of you."

She's smaller than I am, Jill reminded herself. She can't hurt me. She stood up. "Where are my car keys, Diane?"

Diane smiled again and reached into the pocket of her robe. "You mean these?" she said, jingling a set of keys in a black leather key case.

"Give them to me," Jill said.

"If you really want them," Diane said, "get them yourself!" She threw the key case into the fireplace, where it disappeared behind a blazing log.

"All right, then, I'll walk," Jill said, starting for the door. The thought of facing the Fear Street woods again was less frightening than staying with Diane another minute.

"Oh, no, you won't!" cried Diane, running after her. She tackled Jill from behind. Jill felt herself falling forward. She hit the floor hard, the breath rushed out of her. Diane had her hands in Jill's hair and began pulling.

"Stop it!" Jill shrieked. "Leave me alone!" She twisted and struggled and finally managed to turn over. But Diane was on top of her again, scratching and hitting her.

"You always thought I was harmless!" Diane gasped between blows. "Sweet, harmless little Diane! Well, what do you think now?"

"Diane, please stop! Don't!"

Jill had her arms up, trying to fend off the blows, but Diane was amazingly strong and quick. "I took a self-defense course last summer," Diane said smugly.

Desperately, Jill grabbed at Diane's robe to try to pull Diane off her.

Diane didn't move. But the robe fell from Diane's shoulders. Jill stared at Diane and then screamed in horror.

Crisscrossing Diane's body, from her hips to her shoulders, were long, ropy red scars.

chapter
27

*H*er body weak with shock and horror, Jill continued to stare at Diane. Diane stood up, then turned around, almost as if she were modeling a new dress.

The horrible scars continued on her back and the backs of her arms. Jill couldn't even imagine the pain that had produced such hideous scars.

"Seen enough?" Diane asked. "This is what happened to me four years ago. I was visiting my grandmother when her kerosene heater exploded."

"Oh, Diane." Jill could hardly talk. "How horrible!"

"It was horrible, all right," said Diane. "More than you could imagine in a hundred years. There aren't words for the kind of pain I felt."

"I had no idea," Jill went on. "It's hard to believe you're alive."

"I nearly died," Diane said almost proudly. "The doctors all said I didn't have a chance. But I lived, Jill. And do you know why?"

"No," Jill whispered, unable to tear her eyes from the horrifying sight of Diane's scarred torso.

"It was because of Gabe," Diane said intensely. "He came to see me every day. He brought me assignments from school. He played his guitar and sang songs, just for me. He talked to me. He gave me a reason to go on. A reason to want to fight the pain and live."

"You've been in love with him ever since."

"Yes," Diane said simply. "He is my true soulmate. He gave me life." For a moment her eyes filled with tears; then she blinked them away. "I know Gabe loved me too, but of course he never said anything to me. How could he?"

"I'm sure he cares for you," said Jill, suddenly realizing that her friend was living in a fantasy world where Gabe was her knight in shining armor.

"I know. But we can never be together. My body is ruined. It can never be! *It can't be!*" Diane shouted, her face twisted with rage. "I've told him that a hundred times!"

Had she really? Jill wondered. Or was this something she had made up in her madness?

"I know what you're thinking," Diane went on. "You think I'm just imagining that Gabe loves me. That I'm jealous of you and Andrea. Well, you're partly right." She fixed her blue eyes on Jill and spoke slowly and intently. "I can't ever be Gabe's girlfriend, as I told you. But if I can't have him, neither can anyone else—not Andrea and not you, Miss Perfect!"

Bracing for another attack, Jill rolled away as far as she could. But Diane didn't rush at her again. Instead, she went on talking, and Jill listened, at once horrified and fascinated by the things she was hearing.

"Oh, Jill," Diane said. "You're so innocent, almost a baby, really. You don't know anything at all, and you won't—until you have experienced real pain."

"Diane," Jill said gently. "It's not too late for you. You can still get help. I'll go with you to a counselor. Maybe there's a plastic surgeon in New York or someplace—"

Diane laughed bitterly. "Don't try to kid me, Jill! Nobody can fix *this!*" She looked down at her body with obvious loathing. "When the boys started their little competition with the fire, you thought it was just fun and games, didn't you?" When Jill didn't answer, she pressed, "Didn't you?"

"Yes," Jill admitted. "But—"

"You didn't realize," Diane went on, "that fire is a very serious thing. Well, now I'm going to show you just how serious it can be!"

With a sudden motion Diane slipped her robe back on, and then, before Jill could move or say anything, she reached back to her father's workbench and grabbed his blowtorch.

"No!" Jill cried, pulling herself to her feet in panic.

But Diane ran past her and stood directly in front of the cabin door. "This is how I started the fire on Fear Street. It was a beautiful fire." She smiled in a dreamy way as she switched the torch on.

Then she aimed it directly at Jill.

chapter

28

"No!" Jill screamed again. She twisted away from Diane and stumbled into the couch. "No! Diane, stop!"

But Diane was right behind her. The couch burst into flames.

Choking on the acrid smoke, Jill ran across the room. She tried to open the window, but it was painted shut. The curtains began to blaze. She twisted away from the searing heat.

Diane was just behind her, laughing maniacally, touching the flame to every object Jill came near. Everything in the cabin was smoldering now.

Gasping from the smoke and superheated air, Jill tried again to reach the cabin door. Diane's jacket, which she was still wearing, caught fire, and she ripped it off in panic.

"Not that way, Jill," said Diane, aiming the blowtorch in her path.

Jill broke away and rushed for the kitchen area.

In the sink sat a big pan full of soapy water.

Without even thinking, Jill grabbed the pan and threw it at Diane. It hit her in the shoulder and drenched her robe. But it didn't even touch the glowing flame of the blowtorch.

"Nice try, Jill," sneered Diane. "But you'll never get away from me now."

Again she aimed the torch at Jill, and again Jill spun away.

"Feel the pain, Jill!" Diane cried. "Feel the pain!"

Jill could feel the blowtorch singe her hair. She screamed and lunged forward, tripping over the ottoman. She fell hard and lay there, trying to catch her breath.

Diane was standing above her now, her face blank with madness, everything in the cabin blazing around her.

She brought the torch down slowly, directly at Jill's face.

Jill shut her eyes in terror, feeling the scorching heat move closer.

And closer.

I'm gone, she thought.

I'm gone.

Then, suddenly, the cabin door burst open.

A blast of cool, cool air blew through the cabin.

"That's enough!" cried a strong, masculine voice.

It was Gabe.

"Do you hear me?" he shouted. "Stop, Diane! Stop now!"

Dazed, Jill watched through the smoke as he grabbed for the torch.

Diane pulled away, surprisingly quick, and Gabe let

out a cry of pain as the flame burned his hand. For an endless moment they struggled, Gabe and Diane. Then finally Gabe wrestled the torch from her hand and threw it down.

"Nooo!" Diane wailed. "Noooo!"

Gabe took Diane by the shoulders and pushed her through the flames and smoke out the door. An instant later he returned and pulled Jill outside. He rolled her over and over on the ground, extinguishing the flames that had begun to catch onto her clothes.

"Are you all right?" he asked at last. His eyebrows were singed, and thick, sooty smoke covered his handsome face.

"I think so," Jill whispered.

Without another word, Gabe turned to Diane, who was kneeling on the cabin lawn, her body shaking with silent sobs. Tenderly Gabe put his arms around her and held her.

Giant flames poured out of the cabin now, and Jill could hear the faint sound of sirens in the distance.

Still holding Diane, Gabe stared at the fire. He began to speak, almost as if to himself.

"Andrea called me," he said. "She told me where you were, Jill. She was afraid you wouldn't believe her."

"I almost didn't," Jill admitted.

His face unbearably sad, Gabe went on, now stroking Diane's hair as he held her close. "Poor Diane. That fire was so long ago. I guess I didn't really want to remember how scared and sick she was. I used to bring her her homework. Her parents said I helped her. So I came. But now my stupid fire game has caused *this.*"

Jill continued to look at Gabe and Diane, silhouetted by the fire. Gabe was still talking, but not to Jill.

Instead, he was tenderly speaking to Diane, telling her again and again, "It's over, Diane. The fire game is over. It's over for good."

About the Author

R. L. STINE is the author of nearly twenty bestselling mysteries and thrillers for Young Adult readers. He also writes funny novels, joke books, and books for younger readers.

In addition to his publishing work, he is Head Writer of the children's TV show, "Eureeka's Castle."

He lives in New York City with his wife, Jane, and son, Matt.

THERE IS NO VACATION FROM THE TERRORS OF *FEAR STREET*®

Next . . .

PARTY SUMMER

Available as an Archway book

Cari Taylor and her three friends look forward to a "party summer" working at The Howling Wolf Inn, an old hotel on a tiny island off Cape Cod. But to their dismay, the hotel is completely deserted, and they are warned to leave immediately.

The mysterious owner, Simon Fear III, allows Cari and her friends to stay, giving them the run of the hotel. The four teenagers are thrilled until they realize they have been put up in the "haunted wing" . . . until Simon's weird and frightening brother appears . . . until they hear a woman screaming, "No party—please, no party!"

When Simon Fear is murdered, Cari and her horrified friends want out. But they can't escape! They're trapped on the island. And *that's* when the "party" begins. . . .